SHAYLA CHERRY

Big Island Sunrise

Copyright © 2023 by Shayla Cherry

All rights reserved. No part of this publication may be reproduced, stored or transmitted in any form or by any means, electronic, mechanical, photocopying, recording, scanning, or otherwise without written permission from the publisher. It is illegal to copy this book, post it to a website, or distribute it by any other means without permission.

This novel is entirely a work of fiction. The names, characters and incidents portrayed in it are the work of the author's imagination. Any resemblance to actual persons, living or dead, events or localities is entirely coincidental.

Shayla Cherry has no responsibility for the persistence or accuracy of URLs for external or third-party Internet Websites referred to in this publication and does not guarantee that any content on such Websites is, or will remain, accurate or appropriate.

First edition

This book was professionally typeset on Reedsy. Find out more at reedsy.com

Contents

1	Lani	1
2	Emma	10
3	Lani	16
4	Emma	27
5	Lani	33
6	Emma	41
7	Lani	52
8	Emma	60
9	Lani	71
10	Emma	80
11	Lani	87
12	Emma	96
13	Lani	104
14	Emma	112
15	Lani	124
16	Emma	133
17	Lani	140
18	Emma	150
19	Lani	160
20	Emma	169
21	Lani	176
22	Emma	184
23	Lani	189
24	Emma	196

25	Lani	205
26	Emma	217
27	Lani	225
28	Emma	234
29	Tara	241
Acknowledgments		248

1

Lani

"Welcome to Hilo, folks." The pilot's voice crackled over the speakers. "The local time is 3:27pm, and the temperature is seventy-five degrees Fahrenheit."

While other passengers crowded the aisle, Lani stared out at the Big Island's lush greenery and pearl-gray skies. Tears of relief coursed down her face, mirroring the droplets of water that ran down the outside of the airplane window.

She'd finally made it. She'd escaped.

She was home.

Lani dried her tears and looked down at her daughter.

Rory was curled up with her head in her mama's lap, sound asleep. The four year old had made it through a predawn departure, two layovers, and two of three flights with her eyes wide open. Finally, on the short flight from Kahului to Hilo, she had fallen asleep.

Lani gently shook her daughter's shoulder to try and wake her, but Rory just muttered something and curled into a tighter ball. So Lani squeezed past her and pulled their carry-on down from the overhead bin, then slung her backpack over her shoulders before picking up her little girl.

Her first breath of island air smelled like home. The warm breeze moved over her skin like a balm.

All around her, tourists were wilting and panting in the mild heat.

She just breathed deeper, relishing the moisture in the air. It ran gently through her body, soaking into her every cell.

"Leilani!" Her family was waiting for her at the curb, eyes filled with tears at the joy of seeing her again. Auntie Mahina looked so much like her mom that it made her heart ache.

With Lani's mother and Uncle John both gone, Mahina was the only Kealoha sibling left standing. She was the matriarch and the axis of her extended family. All those years away, and she still pulled Lani back into the spinning circle of their *'ohana* like no time had passed.

Alongside her relief, Lani felt a rush of shame that she had stayed away for so long, far from all of these people who loved her and welcomed her back with open arms.

"Look at you!" Mahina exclaimed. "Look at this *baby*, she's beautiful!"

Half awake, Rory clung to her mama and stared wide-eyed at the aunties she had only ever seen through a screen. She buried her face in Lani's shoulder as their family enveloped them with hugs and caresses.

As the love of her family washed over her, grief mixed with gratitude and released a flood of tears that she couldn't hold back. They flowed silently down her cheeks and into her daughter's hair.

Here in the warmth of Hawai'i, Alaska felt so far away. Like someone else's story.

There, she had filled her house with potted plants and artificial lights to get through the maddening darkness of winter.

Here, the tropical plants that she had kept indoors grew wild. As they drove south from the airport, she stared out the window at houseplants the size of houses.

It felt like she was traveling back through time to early childhood. By the time she was a teenager, all of the marvels of this place seemed ordinary. Now, after years spent off island, the greenery and tropical air felt miraculous again.

"Mama, I need to pee." Rory was strapped into a borrowed car seat between Lani and her cousin. She wiggled and rubbed her eyes, still fighting sleep.

Lani bit her lip and frowned. "I'm sorry, baby. I should have asked before we got in the car."

"We've got another half hour to go," Mahina said from the driver's seat.

"It's a pee-mergency," Rory said in an urgent whisper.

"Take the next exit," said Mahina's daughter, 'Ōlena. "There's a bathroom at the park."

"Thank you," Lani said. "Sorry, I should know better."

"You have nothing to apologize for." 'Ōlena was beautiful, with thick black hair and glass-brown eyes. She had always been bigger than Lani, tall and strong.

With an ancestry that was more Portuguese and Japanese than Hawaiian, Lani had always felt out of place around her cousins. She felt slightly out of place wherever she went, truth be told. Ethnically ambiguous, her father had called it, always with that wry smile he had. She was rarely glaringly out of place, but she never quite fit in either.

"Two minutes, Rory," Mahina said from up front. "Can you hold it?"

"Okay." Her perfect little face pulled together with determination.

"What sort of name is Rory anyway?" an old auntie asked from the front seat. Lani was too embarrassed to admit that she didn't remember her name. She wasn't even a hundred percent sure of who she was, though she was thinking it must be Mahina's mother-in-law. "It sounds like a mouthful of peanut butter."

"Mom!" Mahina admonished. "It does not."

"Her full name is Aurora," Lani explained, holding her daughter's hand. "For the northern lights."

Aurora Borealis – it had felt like the perfect name at that moment, caught up in the lovestruck haze of holding her baby girl for the first time. All through her labor, lime green and amethyst lights had danced just outside the window.

In retrospect, the name was overkill. But Rory suited her well enough.

"Well I guess that's pretty. At least it means something. A name should mean something."

After a quick bathroom stop and a few trips down a hot plastic side, they were on the road again. Lani and Rory would be staying with Mahina until they found a place of their own – no small task in Hawai'i, where more and more of the houses were being turned into vacation rentals for tourists. But their extended family was big, and the family's network of friends and acquaintances was larger still. They would find something eventually.

There were rainbows everywhere – on every license plate, appearing and disappearing in massive double arcs between the shifting clouds. Rory exclaimed over each one, voicing Lani's newfound awe.

In all her years away, Lani hadn't let herself think about how much she missed this place. Now that homesickness caught up with her in a mad rush. Her lungs ached with it, desperately missing the place that she was right in the middle of. She breathed steadily and let it wash over her.

She had expected it, this assault of emotion that came with coming home again. It was one reason she had stayed away for so long.

When her parents died, they left behind a gaping hole of grief that made the island uninhabitable. To be there without them was unthinkable.

And yet, here she was. And here was her island, green and gorgeous as ever. And her family, what was left of it, willing and eager to take them in.

The green stretch of highway took them south from Hilo and past the small town of Kea'au before they finally pulled off the main road and turned towards Pualena.

The town was just as she remembered it, a single commercial road with a handful of restaurants and galleries that catered to locals and tourists who liked to explore off the beaten trail. She caught sight of the Pualena Cafe and her cousin Kekoa's new shave ice place before the car turned off the main road.

There were cars everywhere when they drove up to the family compound, and Lani braced herself for a mad rush of cousins and neighbors.

Auntie Mahina and her husband Manō had raised their kids there, and two of them still lived on the property. 'Ōlena and her daughters lived in the main house with her parents. Kekoa lived towards the back of the lot in the house that he had built himself.

"Hey sis." Kekoa pulled her into a bear hug as soon as he saw her. "Long time no see."

"Leilani!" Manō shouldered past his son and lifted her into a hug.

Mahina's husband was even bigger than his sons, a bear of a man. Never once had Lani heard him raise his voice in anger at his kids or anyone else. He didn't have to. When Manō spoke, everyone listened.

"Hey Uncle," she said, hugging him.

"How you doing?" His heavy local accent washed over her, warm and welcome as the ocean breeze. "You still work them cruise ships?"

"She hasn't been on a ship in years," 'Ōlena told her dad. "Not since her baby was born."

"Not such a baby anymore! Look at that face, she growing up. You hungry, Rory?"

Rory pressed her face against Lani's leg, and she gave her uncle an apologetic smile. "She's shy."

"Shy's okay." He grinned and slapped her on the back. "We glad to have you home. *E komo mai.*"

Beyond the nucleus of her family, dozens of others were waiting to greet her.

Lani understood her daughter's overwhelm. She was a grown-up, and even she was wishing that she could just hide her face and wait for the crowd to clear.

She kept up as best as she could, unsure of who half of them were, whether they were second and third cousins or just the kind of 'cousins' that had grown up in the neighborhood.

"Come on tru," Manō said, "make house, we got food on da *lanai*. You got one job yet?"

"Oh my God, Dad." 'Ōlena gave her a wide-eyed look of apology. "Enough already. She's not even inside yet, stop grilling her."

"I not grillin, I just askin."

"Nothing lined up yet," Lani admitted.

"Kekoa has somethin." He looked expectantly at his son.

"We could use someone at the shave ice place," Kekoa said. "It's just a cashier job."

"Sure," Lani said. "Thank you so much. I'll take anything. I just have to figure out something for Rory."

"'Ōlena can take her with all the other *keiki*," said Manō. *Da udda*, he said, the *th-* sound morphing to *d*. His voice made her heart ache with the knowledge that she was finally home. Her cousins spoke with a similar accent, though not as strongly as their dad.

"I run a daycare," 'Ōlena confirmed. "The kids are pretty much always outside, it's great."

"Thank you," Lani managed, half choked with gratitude for how everyone was going out of their way to give her and Rory a soft landing.

"You home now," Uncle Manō said, one massive hand eclipsing her shoulder. "You got nothing for worry about."

She nodded quickly, swallowing back another thank you along with her tears.

"It's a co-op," 'Ōlena told her quietly. "Anyone who can't pay, or can't pay the full amount, contributes in other ways. Usually by staying one or two days a week to help watch the kids. So you can do that to start. It will be a great way to help Rory get used to everything."

"That sounds perfect. Thank you."

They brought her to a table out on the *lanai* and gave her a plate heaped with sticky white rice and *lau lau*. No doubt the taro leaves wrapped around the meat had come from Mahina's garden. Chances were that the family had caught the fish and killed the pig themselves or knew the people who had. It was pure island comfort food.

Once her stomach was full, she was fighting to keep her eyes open. It was still light outside, the sky streaked orange and pink as the sun set on the other side of the island, but Rory was sound asleep in her lap.

"All *pau*?" Mahina asked, clearing her plate away. "'Ōlena, show Leilani where her and Rory go sleep."

"There's space for Rory in the girls' room," 'Ōlena said as she led her through the house, "but I figured she'd want to sleep with you. We put an air mattress in the office. I'm sorry there's not a real bedroom free, but between me and the girls—"

"This is great, 'Ōlena. I'm so grateful just to have a place to land." The bed was all made up, and someone had put her luggage in the opposite corner. The space was small, but it was *safe* – something that Lani would never take for granted again. "I'm so glad to be home."

"We're glad to have you." She gave her another tight squeeze. "My girls are with their dad today, but they're going to be so excited to see Rory. Come find me if you need anything. Bathroom's just one door down."

Lani tried to set Rory on the bed without waking her, but her baby girl stirred as soon as she put her down. Worry flickered over her face. Then her eyes found Lani, and she relaxed.

"Hi, Mama." She smiled sleepily. "Is this our new house?"

"For a little while." She squeezed onto the bed and smiled as her daughter's tiny fingers traced the curve of her cheek. Rory blinked slowly, settling back towards sleep.

"I like your face like this," she said.

"Like what, baby?"

"Happy." Rory's eyes drifted shut. "No bruises."

A wave of emotion slammed into her, catching her off guard.

The things that her baby had witnessed this past year were seared into her conscience. She put a protective hand on Rory's back. As she drifted off to sleep, Lani made a silent promise.

Never again.

She had finally found the strength to bring her daughter home. They would make a fresh start here. And no matter what happened, she wouldn't let him drag them back into the mess they'd left behind.

2

Emma

Hilo was quiet.

It had rained all night, and soon the bayfront town would be filled with birdsong and traffic. But now, just for a moment, there seemed to be no sound at all.

Thick fog hung all around, and the whole building was shrouded in mist. Even the trees a few feet away were hazy and gray. It gave everything an otherworldly quality.

Emma sat on the hotel balcony. The sliding glass door was cracked open so that she could hear her son when he woke up. She had a hot cup of coffee between her hands and a blanket around her shoulders, but she still felt cold.

She was always cold.

Grief had taken hold of her body like a chronic illness. It had settled into her bones, an interminable ache and leaden weight. Food repelled her. Sleep eluded her at night, only for her to collapse into bed midafternoon and sleep for hours.

When she looked in the mirror, she hardly recognized herself. Her skin had taken on a grayish hue. Grief had dimmed the light in her eyes and carved dark circles beneath them. Even her auburn hair had lost its shine.

They had come to the Big Island to deal with an inheritance. At least, that was what Emma had told her family. And it was true that she needed to figure out what to do with the land that her six-year-old son had inherited. But it was also true that she had desperately needed to get away from her hometown.

She had needed to escape the house where Adam wasn't.

She'd also needed a break from the suffocating sympathy of her family, from friends who were getting on with their lives as if nothing had happened and acquaintances who stopped her in the street to tell her what a hero her husband was, how grateful they were to him and his team for containing the awful wildfire that had nearly destroyed their homes.

As if she cared.

She would gladly see every building reduced to ash if that could bring her husband back.

Worthless, futile thoughts.

Emma shook herself and sat up straighter. She took a long sip of coffee.

She had to keep moving forward. One blind, stumbling step at a time.

With his dad gone, Kai needed her more than ever.

For months she had been a shell of herself, failing to show up for him in even the most basic ways. Her family had picked up the slack, making sure that there was food on the table, seeing that the trash went out, reminding both of them to eat and bathe and sleep.

Enough was enough.

For the first time in her life, she had to learn how to function on her own.

Emma and Adam were teenagers when they fell in love. She had gone straight from her parent's house into Adam's arms. And, despite everyone's assumptions that their romance would flare and fade, it never had. Adam was it for her.

And Adam was gone.

How many times would she have to say that to herself before it felt like a fact? It was still a hollow, impossible thing. A nightmare that refused to fade.

But he was. He was gone, and she was here, and she just had to learn how to live with that.

It was the *how* that she was still figuring out.

Adam's father had only outlived him by a few weeks. When he died, his property went to his only grandson under the condition that Emma would be responsible for it until Kai turned eighteen.

Kai hadn't just inherited land. There were animals that needed to be cared for or rehomed, bills and property taxes to be dealt with. The family had been patient with her in the wake of Adam's death, but there were decisions that needed to be made. And when Adam's aunt wrote to her, asking them to come for John's memorial service and stay a while to untangle Kai's inheritance, the idea of Hawai'i had felt like a lighthouse in the distance.

She couldn't see where she was going. Not yet.

But it at least gave her some direction through the fog of her grief.

"Mom?" Kai's voice went from sleepy to panicked in an instant. "*MAMA?!*"

"I'm here." She pushed the door open wider and stepped into the dim cave of the hotel room.

"Hi." He sank back into the pillows, right back to sleepy. She sat on the edge of the bed and pushed his hair out of his eyes. He was long overdue for a haircut.

"Good morning, kiddo."

"Can I watch YouTube?"

Emma flinched inwardly but kept her voice steady as she said, "No, not just yet."

He made an overblown sound of disappointment and pushed her hand away. She sighed and stood, picked up the room service menu and looked at it without really reading it.

"Are you hungry?" she asked.

"No!" He burrowed beneath the covers. "I want to watch YouTube!"

She let the menu fall from her hand and drifted back to the balcony.

When Kai was a baby, she wouldn't even allow him to be in the same room as a television set. She'd maintained a strict no-screens policy for years.

Eventually she had eased up, and good educational shows had worked their way in slowly, heartwarming stories and beautiful art and animal facts galore. They had used them as a jumping-off point for other things.

Life was different then.

Even the light was different, golden sun streaming through the kitchen windows.

Adam would come home from a shift and they'd throw themselves at him, eager to pull him down the rabbit hole of whatever they were exploring that week, show him the square numbers that Kai was building with magnatiles or the new books they had read ten times over.

The past few months, it was every man for himself. Kai watched endless hours of YouTube videos that sucked him into the blocky, low-res world of Minecraft. And Emma counted the day as a success if he was still alive and fed by the end of it.

It seemed like trying for anything else, like getting out the door to the library or their homeschool group, just ended in a screaming fit or tears.

And she didn't have the energy for any of it.

She knew that parenting was all about connection. She knew what her son needed: unconditional love, empathy, and steady boundaries that gave him a feeling of predictability and safety.

She just didn't have anything left to give.

He needed her to be twice the parent she had been before. Instead she was a shell of herself, disconnected and impatient.

Some coherent corner of her mind knew that all of her small slip-ups day after day were making things worse, leaving him feeling more lost and alone in his grief than ever, but she didn't know how to claw her way back from where she was now.

That's why they were here. A fresh start, away from their house haunted with memories and the deadening routines they had fallen into.

"Do you want to go for a walk?" she asked through the open door.

"No!"

"Why not?"

Kai poked his head out of the blankets and glared suspiciously at the white mist that drifted across the balcony. "We're *in a cloud.*"

"It'll burn off soon." Emma's voice was chipper, but she couldn't keep it up for long. It was impossible to keep her own spirits up, never mind shift the stormy expression on Kai's face.

Well, there was one easy way.

"You can watch TV for a little while," she told him, "and then we'll walk to get some breakfast."

He didn't even hear the second part. He was too busy puzzling out the remote and the novel experience of a television set with channels.

Emma drifted back to the balcony railing, drinking her now-tepid coffee. They were three stories up, surrounded by leaves.

The fog was already thinning out; she could see a bit further than before.

They would walk into town to find breakfast and a few basic groceries. Her car was due to arrive today, and she had booked a hotel walking distance from the portside lot where she had to go to pick it up.

And after that... well. A new challenge.

A fresh start.

3

Lani

"Okay, everybody got their towels?" 'Ōlena kept her eyes on the kids as she lifted overstuffed beach bags out of the back of the car. "Lulu, where's your water bottle? I can't carry everything. Towels and water bottles, come on."

"Where are we?" Rory clung tight to her mother's leg.

"Keiki Beach." Lani lifted the cooler carefully out of the truck, moving in slow motion to make sure she didn't clock any of the kids with the oversized rectangle.

"I don't see a beach."

"It's just there on the other side of that wall. No!" She hooked her daughter back with one leg just as a car drove by. "You wait for me or Auntie 'Ōlena."

"All good?" 'Ōlena said. "We got everything?"

"I think so, yeah."

"Okay, let's go. Luana, you hold hands with the little girls."

"But I have a water bottle and a towel!" she whined.

"Figure it out, Lulu. Water bottle under your arm, there you go. No cars, here's your chance."

It was early in the day and still quiet at the beach park.

A long rock wall protected the little lagoon from incoming waves, creating the perfect sheltered beach for families. The water was low this morning, and the few people there were enjoying the strip of sand that disappeared completely beneath the water at high tide.

"Look, Kacie and her mom are already here. And Olivia's with them."

'Ōlena pointed out their friends and the girls ran off, still hand in hand. She claimed one of the picnic tables and spread plastic-bottomed blankets on the damp green lawn, claiming the space that her co-op would need for their beach day.

The girls were already down in the sand, building castles and walls against the oncoming tide.

"Mama, look what I found!" Rory ran up the steps and across the grass.

"What is it?"

"It's for you." She put a tiny, perfect shell in Lani's palm.

"I love it."

"You know what?" Rory said with gentle astonishment.

Lani smiled and leaned in. "What?"

"I don't miss Daddy at all."

Lani's pulse jumped and sped. Non sequiturs were par for the course with a four year old, but any mention of Zeke still sent her spinning.

She was quiet, not wanting her baby to hear any distress in her voice. Rory was only four, but she was so perceptive that it shocked her at times. She should feel relief that moving away hadn't traumatized her, but instead she felt a deep grief that her daughter didn't have a father figure worth missing.

"I like it better when it's just you and me." Rory's wide brown eyes were earnest.

Lani pulled Rory into her lap and hugged her tight. "Me too, baby."

"Do you want to swim with me?"

"I would love to."

They waded out through the crisp, clear water. The lagoon was cooler than the ocean beyond the rocks, fed by fresh water from underground springs. She could feel it seeping up in places, much colder than the salt water from the bay.

Lani stood waist-deep and laughed with delight as she watched Rory swimming underwater, comfortable as a baby dolphin in the Pacific. The countless hours they had spent in that heated pool at the community center back in Alaska had paid off.

Her eyes went up to the glint of the ocean beneath a vast white sky, and she breathed deep. This was a far cry from that cement building and the stench of chlorine.

Two hours later, as the morning clouds gave way to clear blue skies, Lani showered and swapped her bathing suit out for a t-shirt and shorts.

"I should head out," she told her cousin.

"Okay, here." 'Ōlena offered her car keys, but Lani shook her head.

"I can walk."

Her eyes narrowed. "Take my car, Lani."

"It's okay, I can walk. It's not that far."

"It's four miles. You'll get heatstroke walking back this afternoon."

"I want you to have a car in case anything happens."

"What's gonna happen?" 'Ōlena put a hand up. "No, don't

answer that. I've got my mama-sized first aid kit. Georgia's here all day. We're fine. You take my car, and we'll see you after work."

"Okay," she relented. "Thank you so much."

"No more thank yous, sis. Go on." 'Ōlena pressed the car keys into her hand.

"You're leaving?" Rory slammed into her and grabbed two handfuls of fabric, clinging to her t-shirt and shorts.

She gently pried her daughter's hands away and knelt down in front of her. "I start work today, remember?"

"Can I come?"

"You're going to stay here with Auntie 'Ōlena and your cousins. You'll eat some lunch and do some painting and I'll be back before you know it. It's not even a full day, just half."

"We're doing a big art project," 'Ōlena said brightly.

"I don't want to do art," Rory sniffled.

"Look how big the paper is," Lulu said in a tone just like her mom's. "We have every color of paint *and* we have sponges. Look, this one is shaped like a dinosaur!"

She crossed her arms over her chest. "I don't like dinosaurs."

"You do too," Lani said.

"Do you like flowers?" One of the other girls, a little blondie named Olivia, offered up a coveted daisy-shaped sponge. "You can use this one."

Rory sniffed and nodded. She accepted the battered pink daisy and held it over her heart.

"Come on," Olivia coaxed, holding out her hand. She was only a couple years older than Rory. Lani was touched to see how the older girls looked after the little ones.

Rory held the bigger girl's hand and took a tentative step forward.

"Go," 'Ōlena whispered. "She'll be fine."

Walking away, Lani felt equal parts heartbreak and exhilaration. She had been with Rory all day every day for her whole life, and she still didn't feel ready to let that go. But she had to work. And she was beyond grateful to be able to leave her baby in a beautiful place with family.

She had stayed in an unhappy marriage for years because that had been less painful than being away from her daughter every day. Leaving her baby under fluorescent lights in some overcrowded daycare was an option that she refused to consider. But leaving her to paint pictures with her cousins in the shade just steps from the beach... that was bearable.

It was a short drive from the beach park into town... if Pualena could really be called a town. Its commercial center consisted of half a dozen buildings on the main road that led straight from the highway to the coast.

Kekoa's place was easy to find, freshly painted bright colors. A huge wooden sign read *Haumona Shave Ice*. It was still locked up tight, so she called her cousin.

"Lani," he answered, "I was just gonna call you."

"What's up?"

"School called. 'Iolani puked at recess, I have to pick him up."

"Aw man, poor little dude."

"Sorry I can't come in early, but Hector will be there to open in less than an hour. You're smart, you can learn on the job."

"Yeah, no worries. Give 'Iolani a hug for me."

"Shoots."

Lani hung up with a sigh. She was tempted to drive back to the beach, but showing up only to leave again a few minutes later would just make things harder for Rory.

Her stomach rumbled, reminding her that all she had eaten that day was half a papaya. Pualena Cafe was just across the street, so she went over to take a look.

The place was more or less how she remembered it, with wide windows in front and old diner-style booths running along either side of the long, narrow restaurant.

The menu looked like a fifth grader's homework, plain black text on flimsy printer paper. She scanned the offerings as she slid into a booth. Utter lack of design aside, the revamped options looked to be a major improvement over the greasy burgers she remembered.

There was just one server working, and the place was mostly full. By the time he made it over, she knew what she wanted.

"Sorry to keep you waiting," he said brightly.

Face to face with her server, she felt something like regret. The guy was cute as hell, exactly her type. Or he would have been, back in the day when she had time for that sort of thing. He had an easy smile and an ageless face that could have been anywhere between twenty and forty.

"Start you off with a drink?" he asked.

"I'll have a *liliko'i* cane juice and the chipotle taro burger, please."

"Great choice. Do you want cheese on that?"

"Sure." She smiled nervously, waiting for him to run her order to the kitchen, but he stood still. His eyes were fixed on her face.

"You're Lani King." There was a hint of wonder in his voice, like some movie star had walked into the little restaurant.

"Yeah." She held the menu to her chest, suddenly drowning in awkward guilt.

Running into old acquaintances was such a bittersweet part

of coming home, and she felt terrible when she couldn't remember a name. But this was worse. She didn't recognize her server at all.

She racked her brain, running through her high school class, college friends, her *cousin*'s friends... but she had no idea who this guy was.

How could she have forgotten that face? He was gorgeous, with high cheekbones and clear brown eyes. His black hair was pulled into a short ponytail.

"You don't remember me." If he was disappointed, it didn't show. His smile held. If anything, he seemed to be laughing at her.

"No." She shook her head. "I'm so sorry."

"It's okay. I was a couple grades behind you."

"Oh." School, then. She searched her memories and... still nothing.

"We were in the same math class."

It hit her then in a sudden burst of clarity. She knew *exactly* who he was, and as soon as she realized, she wondered how she could have been so blind before. He had grown at least a foot since the last time she had seen him, but his smile was exactly the same.

"Alfie?! I can't believe it. Of course I remember you! You carried me through precalc."

His grin grew wider as he nodded. "That's me."

"You're all grown up. Wow. Alfie Nakamura."

"No one's called me Alfie in a long time."

"What do you go by now? Alfred?"

"Tenn."

"Ten?" Her right eyebrow quirked up. "Like hang ten?"

"Like Tennyson," he told her.

Lani looked at him blankly.

"My full name is Alfred Lord Tennyson Nakamura."

"You're joking." She put a hand up to cover her smile. "You're not joking."

"My mom wrote her dissertation on Tennyson when she was pregnant with me."

"Wow."

"Yeah."

"The Lord is a bit much."

"It's all a bit much," he said wryly. "At fourteen, being Alfred Nakamura was hard enough without letting anyone know about my two middle names. But my friends found out senior year and started calling me Tennyson. I guess I grew into it after a while."

"No kidding." She eyed him appreciatively, then realized what she was doing and looked away with a blush.

"I'll be right back with your cane juice."

"Thanks."

She ran a hand through her hair, still damp from the beach, and forced herself not to stare at him. The restaurant was small, and she was hyper aware of him standing at the kitchen window talking to the crew. She pulled a pencil from her purse and sketched sea life on the back of the menu, her lifelong default destresser.

"You were always an amazing artist." Tenn set down a tall glass of cane juice, and she flipped the menu over self consciously.

"I was just doodling."

"May I?" He reached for the menu, and she let him pick it up. He flipped it over and looked at the mako shark she had sketched. "This is not a *doodle*. This is amazing."

Heat flooded her face, and she took a sip of the icy drink. The sweet-tart taste of passionfruit and raw sugarcane sent a zing of pleasure all the way down to her mitochondria.

"I've been all around the world," she said, more to deflect from his comments about her drawing than anything, "and I have never tasted anything half so delicious as *liliko'i* cane juice."

"Could you draw some things for our new menus?" Tenn was still admiring her mako shark. Those nightmares of the sea were cartoonish to begin with, all big black eyes and gills and needle teeth. It made them fun to draw. But that was just doodling.

She swallowed nervously. "What kinds of things?"

"I don't know." He slid into the booth across from her. "I was thinking it would be cool to have menus that looked like your old math homework, you know? Just covered in art."

She bit back a smile. "Are you serious?"

"Yeah." His bright, dark eyes were so earnest that Lani glanced away. She leaned towards the center of the restaurant, looking nervously at the other tables.

"Are you on the clock? I don't want you to get in trouble."

His grin didn't waver, and neither did his focus. "What do you think?"

"You really want me to design the new menus?"

"Yeah." He held up the thin printed sheet and explained, "They look like this because I've been tweaking the menu almost every day for months. But I think I've got it down now."

"Is this..." She trailed off, looking around the old diner, and then leaned forward. "This is *your* place?"

"It is. I bought it last year."

"Wow. Good for you."

"We'll see. I haven't run it into the ground yet, so that's something." He passed the menu back to her and stood. "I'll grab your burger. Add your contact info to the mako, yeah? I'll email you the text for the menu, and you can turn it into something cool."

"Okay. Thanks, Al–" She caught herself. "Tenn. You prefer Tenn?"

His smile lit up his whole face, and she marveled again at her own blindness in not recognizing him immediately.

"Lani King, you can call me whatever you want."

Her smile stretched her cheeks, which were growing warmer by the second, and she looked down at the table. To give her hands something to do, she started sketching ideas on the front of the menu. Island kine things: breadfruit, sugar cane, a hen with her chicks. In the top corner, she drew a plumeria branch covered in flowers.

Her phone buzzed with a text from an unsaved number, and she opened it.

You won't get away with this.

A chill went through her.

I'm going to the police. I'm telling them that you kidnapped my daughter.

Lani replied with shaking hands: *She's not your daughter.*

The next text that came through was in all caps, and it was mostly expletives. Lani went to block this number too, but not before another text came through.

You owe me.

She blocked the number and set her phone aside, shaking.

"Ulu burger," Tenn announced. He set the plate down and hesitated. "Lani? Are you okay?"

"Yeah. Thanks." She smiled up at him, but it was tense and

tight. "Hey, where's the nearest phone store? I need a new number."

4

Emma

"We're staying *here*?" Kai's face pinched together with distress as he peered through the chain-link fence. They couldn't see much; an overgrown jungle of tropical plants hid the Kealoha house from the street.

"Yep, this is it," Emma told him. "Grandpa John's place."

"He's dead," Kai said in a flat voice.

She took a deep breath and confirmed, "Yeah."

"Like Daddy." He pulled at the vines that wound through the fence.

Her voice failed her. She put a hand on his shoulder and looked around for the neighbor who was supposed to meet them with the keys.

The air was thick and humid, noisy with roosters and music. The dogs next door ran at the fence and barked. They seemed more excited than territorial, but she didn't love that there was nothing but a flimsy fence between them and her little boy.

Ever since Adam's death, a suffocating fear had grown in her chest. Losing her husband was more than she could reasonably bear, but losing her son would literally kill her.

There were nights that she could only sleep with one arm over him. In her dreams, the hand that rested above his chest clutched an outward-facing dagger. Shadowy specters loomed in her nightmares, waiting to take him from her the moment she dropped her guard.

"Sorry to keep you waiting!"

Emma flinched in surprise, her mind lurching back to the present moment.

She hardly remembered how to inhabit her own body anymore. And she hated that.

"Here I come." The next-door neighbor squeezed through her front gate, leaving an entourage of disappointed dogs and goats and geese behind. "I've been using the gate key every day, but the house key took me a while to find. Sorry. I'm Tara."

"Emma." She shook the hand that the neighbor offered. They were the same height, taller than most women.

Tara's dark blond hair was pulled back into a messy bun. She wore an oversized t-shirt and dirty jeans, and she shone in the way a person does when their life is overflowing with love.

She paused at the gate, sorting through a key ring in search of the one she needed.

Two little redheads came creeping along the fence behind her, hand in hand like horror movie twins. Their round, freckled faces regarded Kai with identical curiosity.

"This is Kai," Emma told them. Her son hadn't noticed the other kids yet; he was still peering through the gate.

"Is there a house?" he asked.

Tara laughed. "Yes, there's a house. Let's go take a look." She turned and gave her girls a wry smile when she saw that they had followed her over. "Did you close the gate?"

"Yes," one said with emphasis. The other just rolled her eyes.

They were older than Kai, maybe nine.

"This is Piper and Paige. I have one more, but he's in class right now. Online."

"Cody's *sixteen*," said one of the twins.

"Piper, would you grab Myrtle?"

A pale gray hen was trying to escape through the narrow opening as Tara opened the front gate. Tara's daughter swooped in and scooped her up, cradling the ball of feathers to her chest like a baby while Kai looked on in awe.

"Always that same one, I swear," Tara muttered. She had been taking care of John's animals for weeks, despite having her own menagerie to maintain next door. "Is this all of your bags?"

"This is it." Emma lifted a carry-on bag in each hand, and Tara hefted the one bigger bag that she had packed.

"John had a good setup," Tara said as she led them through.

Her other daughter came through last and latched the gate securely behind them.

The front path snaked through a garden paradise. Great green leaves the size of her son, hot-pink ti plants blooming from tall stalks, deep purple vines crawling through the shadows.

Huge bushy sunflowers grew en masse, and Tara plucked a leaf off one in passing. It was bigger than her outstretched hand.

"These make great fodder, and there are some other trees growing on the property that make for good high-protein feed. They like this pigeon pea too," she said, pointing at another bushy plant. "The girls giving milk get some extra pellets on the stand, but the wethers are fine with just the cut and carry to supplement their weed eating. And some supplements, of course, but we can get into those later. Goats weren't meant to live in the tropics, really, but they do alright. I'm finding that sheep are easier."

It was all that Emma could do to keep up with the woman physically, never mind taking in a thing that she was saying. A mother hen scratched nearby, finding bits of food for her fluffy babies in the dirt. Her black feathers shone green and purple in the sunlight.

"Mom!" Kai ran up, more animated than she had seen him in months. "Look what I found!" He held out his hands to show her two eggs, one sky blue and the other sage green. "It's like an Easter egg hunt every day!" He deposited them carefully in a basket that one of the girls held and then they were off again.

"The joy of free range chickens," Tara said wryly. "They lay everywhere. The ducks too. Luckily the kids make a game of it. My girls can show you how to candle them using a flashlight and do a float test to make sure that they're fresh. But once you find their favorite spots, you can collect every day and be sure of how fresh they are. They love to switch it up, though. Keeps us on our toes. If it weren't for my girls, I'm not sure I'd get any eggs at all."

They walked through the screened-in lanai and into the house, where they dropped the luggage at the foot of the stairs. It was a beautiful Balinesian-style house, all wood and windows, but it had seen better days. Every surface was cluttered with junk, and the sofas were covered in fur.

"I would have cleaned up for you, but it wasn't my place to go through everything. And honestly, I haven't had time. Pauline took some of the animals with her—"

"Pauline?" Emma asked.

"John's girlfriend. You never met her?"

"No." Guilt sank heavy in her stomach as she looked around. Between Adam's work schedule and the chaos of everyday life, they hadn't visited in years. They had made it out once just before Kai's first birthday, and John had visited them once after that. But other than those two visits, there had been nothing but the occasional phone call or photo.

It felt shameful now, that they had let his last few years pass without a visit. They'd thought that they had more time, years and decades left to make up for those busy early years.

"She lived here for... close to five years? She was devastated after John passed, poor thing. They had two little dogs and a cat, and she took them with her."

"Took them where?"

"Arizona. All the animals were hers, really – John was more about the trees – but in the end, the goats weren't reason enough to stay. Not with John gone. Her daughter and grandbabies are over on the mainland, so she went to join them."

"Hey Mom!" One of the girls ran in and set a full basket of eggs on the kitchen counter. "Can we show Kai the trampoline?"

"If that's okay with his mom."

"That's fine," Emma said, playing it cool.

The truth was, seeing Kai running around outside with other kids made her happy to the point of tears. Ever since Adam's death, Kai had withdrawn from all of his friends back home.

Other parents showed up a time or two, offering to take him to meetups on days that Emma couldn't get out of bed. But it was no use. Kai hid in his closet, under her bed, even under the house once. And eventually, people stopped offering.

"Okay if we run through everything now?" Tara asked. "I'm

sorry to rush, it's just that my friend Liam is coming to buy a lamb in about an hour."

"Yeah, that's fine."

"Okay. Well, you'll definitely want to stay in the main house. The *'ohana* unit's in bad shape; I don't think it has any electricity at the moment. The whole place needs some love, to be honest. The orchards and gardens are overgrown. It happens practically overnight here. The cane grass alone can grow four inches a day."

She led Emma through the orchard and back to the goat pen, a generous green area that held five goats. They all came running when they spotted Tara.

"You could let the goats through the orchard if you're careful to keep them off the trees. Or we can put my sheep through with one of my dogs. Have you ever milked a goat?"

Emma eyed them warily, unnerved by their strange serpentine eyes. "I have not."

"No time like the present." She opened the gate, and Emma followed her through.

5

Lani

It was another gray day, soft light filtering through the clouds. The uncles and aunties were gathered on a patch of grass above the ocean, preparing for the memorial service.

Dozens of surfers bobbed below, all jostling for one of the few good breaks on the east side of the island. John had surfed here for decades, and his closest friends and relatives would paddle out past the break today to circle up, say a final goodbye, and spread his ashes.

"So sad to lose John right after Adam," one of the aunties was saying.

Lani hugged herself as the cool breeze picked up, carrying salt spray off the ocean. She stood on the edge of things, only half listening.

"No surprise that he had no fight left," a cousin said. "What's a person got left to live for, when their only *keiki* is gone?"

"He's got that grandbaby, though. Kai?"

"All the way in California."

"He's here. You didn't see? Right down there by the water. Look at him, he's all Kealoha."

"John left everything to him, did you hear?"

"But he's just a baby."

"What's his mother gonna do, rent it out?"

"More land lost to a mainlander. What a shame."

Lani moved away from the gossiping aunties, following Rory as she wandered down the path to the beach. She hadn't seen Adam in years, had never even met his son, but the news of his death had gutted her.

The Kealoha siblings had been close, and Adam was her best friend growing up. Each an only child, the two of them had forged a bond that was closer than siblings – all of the love with none of the bickering.

They had grown apart in adulthood, so busy with their own lives that they rarely saw each other. Then she'd married Zeke, who hated to see any male name on her phone (hated for her to even *have* a phone, really). And by the time she had finally made it home, two more of her closest relatives were gone. The black hole of loss at the center of her island had grown even wider; she was half surprised that she couldn't see it.

Adam should be here.

The sharp pain of his death had catapulted her out of the gray complacency of her life. She wanted Rory to know her cousins. Even if all she had was second cousins, there was really no difference as far as her family was concerned.

Lani's foolishness had robbed Rory of her paternal family, and a cruel twist of fate had taken her grandparents decades too soon. She at least deserved to know her *'ohana*. The family they had left.

Like Lani, Adam had always been slightly outside of the family. His mother was from California, and he had moved back there with her as a young teenager after his parents split. But he had grown up in Pualena, and he'd visited the island every winter break and every summer.

They had only grown closer over the years. He was there for her in the wake of her mother's death. Even when he brought his highschool girlfriend, Emma, they had included Lani on their long hikes and Kona beach days.

Most teenage boys would have cast off a sad, quiet little cousin. But not Adam.

Lani scanned the beach, looking for Emma. They had become as close as sisters, all those summers through high school and college. Lani had even been a bridesmaid in her wedding, standing up there with Emma's two blood sisters. They had stayed in touch during her cruise ship years, and she had gone to visit after Kai was born.

Then came Rory. And Alaska. And a husband who read her every text or deliberately let the phone and internet go unpaid so that she had no contact with the outside world at all.

Lani would put up a front when she did get service, too ashamed to admit what she had gotten herself into. For years, she hadn't even admitted it to herself. It had gotten worse so slowly, during a time when all of her focus was on her baby girl. Before she knew it, the water was hot enough to scald.

She followed Rory down the beach, walking barefoot across the warm black sand.

As they got closer to the river, the sand gave way to smooth stones. A group of young boys had started their own little driftwood bonfire and Rory tiptoed closer, staring at their accomplishment in awe. When they failed to acknowledge her, she lost interest and wandered down to the river's edge.

Lani stayed right behind her, watching carefully. The river pooled here, deep and still as a lake. The water was so clear that she could see all the way to the rocky bottom. But just a short distance to their right, the current was swift and fierce. A group of older kids whooped and hollered, riding the rapids towards the ocean.

"Mama, look!" Rory held up a green bit of sea glass. "Look what I found!"

"That's beautiful, baby!"

Rory gasped. "Oh my goodness! There's another one!"

Before long, they had a pile of sea glass gathered: green and blue and brown. There were even bits of pottery, little shards of blue on white. They were absorbed in collecting those treasures for a long while before Lani finally remembered herself. She stood up and looked around, wondering if the service had already started.

Emma was just a few yards away.

Lani stared at her for a moment, wondering if that was really her. Adam's widow was curled in on herself, gray and tired.

She watched her son carefully as he waded through the water, but there was a hollowness to her expression. She was a woman not quite there, barely tethered to her body. Lani knew that feeling all too well.

"Emma." She put a hand on her shoulder, and Emma gave her a vacant-eyed look. It went on for several beats, long enough for Lani to wonder if she had forgotten her altogether. Then there was a spark of recognition, followed immediately by an upwelling of tears.

"Lani." She pulled her into a crushing hug. "Oh my God, you're so grown up. How long has it been?"

"Long time." She hugged her back just as fiercely, heart breaking for the years she had missed, the time with Adam that she would never be able to make up for now.

But there was Kai.

She pulled back and looked at her little cousin. He stood at the river's edge, watching the current with a serious expression on his face.

"He looks just like Adam."

"I know." Emma swiped tears from her face with the back of her hand, but her eyes brightened with a smile. "Everyone says so. I'm glad we're here. Kai's not so sure."

"He'll come around."

"Mama, look!" Rory ran over, stumbling over the river stones. She held her hands out to show a rare find, a bit of sea glass that was the same bright lime green as the northern lights.

"Beautiful! Rory, this is Emma. She's your auntie."

"*Another* auntie?" Rory looked up at her with wide eyes, and both women laughed.

"Yep, another one." Emma crouched down and pointed at her son. "That's Kai over there. He's your cousin."

"There you are!" Kekoa walked up and clapped Lani on the back. "We're about to paddle out. Are you coming?"

"I need to stay here with Rory," Lani said.

"Emma?"

She shook her head.

"You sure? We have extra boards."

"I can't." Her voice cracked, and he put a gentle hand on her shoulder.

"Okay, no worries. If you change your mind, let me know. We're right up there."

"Thanks, Kekoa."

He nodded and strode back across the beach.

Lani and Emma were quiet as they watched their kids play on the rocky shore of the river. Kai threw stones that vanished instantly into the fast-moving water of the narrow outlet. Rory sat sorting the treasures she had found.

The two kids could have been siblings, they looked so much alike. Round faces, dark hair, huge brown eyes. And beyond that, a solemnity that set them apart from other kids their age. Lani's heart ached for both of them.

"Adam's paddle out was just a few weeks ago," Emma said after a while.

"I'm sorry I couldn't be there." Lani wasn't sure if Emma had even heard her. That lost, vacant look had overtaken her face again.

"I wore his wetsuit. Went out on his board, that old red one that he had so long it turned pink. It was a calm day. Seemed like half the mountain was out there with me. We left most of his ashes out there in the ocean. My sisters kept some for me, put it in this little lacquered box." She trailed off.

Then, with sudden vehemence, she said, "I hate it. My firefighter reduced to ash. It's like a sick joke. But I brought it with me, that bit of him. I couldn't leave it behind. I thought maybe I could... here, with his dad. But I left it in my luggage. I just... couldn't. Not yet."

Lani put a compassionate hand on her arm, and Emma jumped like she was startled to see her standing there. She pressed her lips together into a grim, apologetic smile and sniffed back tears that she hadn't let fall.

"I'm so sorry, Lani. That was too much."

"It's okay. I get it." They walked upriver after their kids, who were wandering towards the calmer bend in the river where other *keiki* were laughing and splashing.

"I don't know how to be normal anymore."

"Normal's overrated." Lani bumped her hip into Emma and saw the shadow of a smile cross her face. "I get it. I do. I didn't even know how to be here with my parents gone. I had to leave the island. Being here without my mom was hard enough. Staying here after my dad died felt impossible. So I got on a ship. Without them, this just didn't feel like home anymore."

"My house feels like a tomb," Emma said so quietly that she could barely hear her. After a moment she asked, "Did it help? Getting away?"

"I don't know," Lani admitted. "I think running away just stretched the hurt out longer. Trying to outrun my pain and being alone, away from family... I made a lot of mistakes. I didn't have guideposts, any mirrors. Family gives us that. Community does." She put an arm around Emma's waist. "But you have family here too. You're not running away."

"My family thinks I am."

"They don't know. Look at Kai." Their two kids stood next to each other now, and Kai was showing Rory how to skip a flat stone across the still water. "Half his family is here. Have you been to the Kealoha place yet?"

"Yeah, we slept there last night."

"How long are you here for?"

"I don't know yet."

Lani turned to look at the paddle out. Her aunt and uncle and cousins were barely visible, part of a bobbing circle far out beyond the breaking waves, saying goodbye to John. "There was a big stink about the paddle out, did you know?"

"What do you mean?"

"The older uncles wanted something more traditional. There was a spot for John in the cemetery near his parents... and mine."

"Are paddle outs not traditional?" Emma asked. "We all paddled out together years ago for a friend of Adam's, remember? He always said that he would want that over a funeral."

"Surfers have been doing paddle outs for over a hundred years, but it's not exactly an ancient tradition. Cremation was more of a punishment than an honor back in the day, and some of the older uncles are upset that he won't be in the cemetery with his parents. But this is what he wanted. To join Adam in the Pacific."

There was a comforting continuity to the ocean. Lani had always felt it on the ships, and in Alaska. However many thousands of miles she might be from Hawai'i, so long as she was by the ocean, she wasn't too far from home.

Next to her, Emma wiped her eyes and nose with the corner of a beach towel. They walked closer to where the kids played and settled down in the sand.

They sat like that for a long time, shoulder to shoulder, with their back to the memorial and their faces towards the sun.

6

Emma

Emma felt as if she had been handed the captainship of a boat without having the faintest idea of where it was headed or how to get there.

Just milking the goats in the morning, which had taken Tara less than twenty minutes, took her nearly two hours.

Tara had offered to help her find homes for the many animals that lived on the Kealoha property. Emma just had to keep them alive and well in the meantime.

Having seen to the goats, she went back inside to strain their milk and put it in the fridge.

"Can I have some?" Kai asked.

"Of course."

She looked at the table and realized that he had found her phone and pulled up YouTube videos while she was outside. Pretty impressive for a kid who was still learning how to read.

"No more videos," she said as she poured him a glass of raw milk.

Kai's expression darkened into a belligerent scowl. "Why

not?"

"It's a beautiful day."

"There's nothing to do."

"There's plenty to do."

"There's no one to play with."

"What about Paige and Piper next door?"

Kai considered this for a moment. He drank the milk in one go, and she felt a rush of gratitude. He had been a picky eater to begin with, and that had grown steadily worse in the months since his father's death. It was a comfort to be able to give him as much farm fresh milk as he could drink.

"How do I get past the fence?" he asked.

"I'll walk with you. Let's go see if they're home."

They walked through the lush jungle that was the Kealoha front yard, every shade of green punctuated with bursts of pink and yellow and red. She led him out the front gate and around to the neighbors' place, where they both flinched back from the immediate, earsplitting alarm that was the barking and baying of Tara's two farm dogs.

One of the twins ran to the gate, and her smile fell into a more neutral expression when she saw who it was.

"Oh, it's just you."

"Piper, don't be rude." Tara smiled apologetically and set down the buckets that she was carrying. The dogs quieted as she approached the gate, and the barking faded to whines of greeting. "What's up?"

"We were wondering if the girls wanted to come play," Emma said.

"We're busy today," Piper told her.

Tara gave her a warning look. "We have some friends coming over today. Kai is welcome to join."

He looked uncertainly at Piper, who shrugged.

"Want to come play on the trampoline?" she asked.

He nodded vigorously and bolted through the gate the moment that Tara cracked it open. She closed it immediately after him, pulling a curious goat away from the opening as she did so.

"How's it going over there?" Tara asked over the top of the gate.

Emma held her hands out in an exaggerated shrug. "Nobody's died yet."

"Well, it's only a matter of time." She laughed at Emma's expression and added, "It's a fact of farm life, I'm afraid. But you're doing all right?"

She spread her hands again. "I managed to milk the goats in two hours this morning. Took me three last night."

Tara grinned. "You'll get the hang of it. Let me know if you need help with anything in particular."

Her husband shouted from the front door, asking what she had done with his laptop, and the goats joined in his bleating.

"I'll let you go," said Emma.

"Sorry, it's a madhouse over here. Kai is welcome to stay as long as he likes. We have a bunch of kids from our homeschool co-op coming by later. They'll be here most of the day."

"Okay, thank you."

She circled back to the Kealoha property and walked slowly through the yard, unsure of what to do next. She felt as though she were standing at the bottom of a mountain. She had a vague sense of where she was going but only the foggiest idea of how to get there.

She went inside to pour herself another cup of coffee and stood looking around the cluttered kitchen.

There were tchotchkes everywhere, magnets from various states all over the fridge, so many plastic cups and bowls and commemorative mugs that they spilled out of the cupboards and onto the counters. A lot of junk that John's girlfriend hadn't bothered to take with her.

That seemed as good a place to start as any.

She knew from her many summers on the island that each of the transfer stations where people took their trash also had donation bins and areas where everything worth saving was sold off at a bargain. And so, starting with the kitchen, she began collecting all of the clutter and piling it into the back of her car.

That was the easiest place to start, because there was nothing in there of obvious sentimental value. She collected dozens of mugs and bowls and piles of mismatched silverware and put them all into bags and boxes. She cleared most of the magnets off of the old refrigerator and then began going through the food. Most of it needed to be thrown away, but there were also large amounts of canned food and other salvageable things that she could drop off at the nearest food bank.

She followed this decluttering of the kitchen with a deep clean. The whole process ate up half of the day and left her with a satisfying feeling of accomplishment. One room down. One place in the house that she could use every day without feeling crowded out and overwhelmed.

She checked on Kai through the fence and saw him feasting on a platter of homegrown fruits and vegetables that Tara had put out. It was mostly stuff that he would have refused to touch at home, but between the hunger-inducing exercise of a morning on the trampoline and the fact that the twins were happily eating their fruits of their mother's labor, Kai was content to snack on carrots and starfruit.

Emma went back inside and looked around, wondering what to tackle next. She walked to the back of the living room, to shelves with a sparse smattering of pictures, gap-toothed from all of the photos that John's girlfriend had taken with her to Arizona.

All that remained were photos of the Kealohas. Adam was in most of them. She lifted one off the shelf for a closer look at Adam when he was about seven or eight.

He looked just like Kai. Of course, the reverse was true, but that was her first thought anytime she saw an old photo of her husband.

It broke her heart all over again that Kai hadn't gotten the chance to know his grandfather. Losing John while they were still grieving Adam was an insult on top of a near-fatal injury to their little family.

Emma could feel herself sinking back into that pit where she had lived for months, her energy seeping quickly away.

She turned and marched back outside, determined to escape the rip current of grief.

"What needs doing?" she wondered aloud.

She surveyed the lush green acreage. The grass in the orchard was half as high as the trees. At the rate that this invasive grass grew in Hawai'i, she only had to turn around and the grass and vines would overtake the fruit trees entirely. The jungle was like that, always ready to reclaim its territory at the slightest lapse in attention.

She marched over to the toolshed and surveyed her options with a slight sense of trepidation. She disliked power tools and had an aversion to weed whackers and lawn mowers that bordered on fear. Mostly she found the sound of them overwhelming. But she wasn't certain of her ability to control them either.

She opted for a hand scythe, a large crescent blade attached to a comfortable handle. So armed, she marched back out to face the overgrown grass. This section was nearly six feet tall, broad blades on round stalks broader than her fingers.

When she grabbed a handful of the huge stalks, pain exploded through her palm and fingers.

She released them with a yelp of surprise. The hand scythe dropped to the ground and disappeared in the tall grass. She examined her left hand and saw that it was full of tiny colorless spines, fierce needles that bit into her skin.

"Cactus grass," came a voice from nearby.

She looked around and saw a woman regarding her over the overgrown fence line. Not Tara on the right, but the neighbor on the left whom she had yet to meet.

"Cactus grass," the woman said again when Emma didn't reply. "Some call it cane grass or elephant grass. Grows a foot a week, easy. You can't touch it without gloves, and even then it works its way through."

Still holding her hand palm up as if in supplication, Emma approached the fence.

"You're the new owner?" the neighbor asked. She was middle-aged with gray hair pulled into a severe bun, and she regarded Emma with equal parts annoyance and amusement.

"Not exactly. John left this property to my son, Kai. His grandson. But he's only six, so—"

"But you're the one responsible?"

"Yes."

"I've been telling John for years about this fence, but he never did a thing about it. Look at how these vines from your side are bringing it down. It's useless now. The whole thing has to be replaced."

Emma stared at her, not quite comprehending. "You want me to fix the fence?"

"I just told you, there's no fixing it. You'll have to clear these vines and the crumpled chain-link and start fresh."

"Right." Emma's hand prickled with pain at the slightest movement. The tiny spines seemed to be working their way deeper into her skin. "I'm just gonna go take care of this, if you don't mind. It was good to meet you."

The woman harrumphed and returned to her garden.

She still hadn't fully unpacked, and it took ten minutes to sort through her luggage one-handed and find a pair of tweezers. It took another ten to carefully pick out the biggest spines, which did little to dull the pain in her hand.

Most of the spines were still in there, either broken off under the skin or so tiny that she couldn't see them. She could feel them, though. They radiated a burning, prickling pain that intensified when she moved her fingers.

A sudden shouting started up outside, and she went to see what the commotion was.

"Back! Get out, you hell beasts! Out!"

She followed the noise and saw her neighbor on the other side of the collapsed wire fencing. It appeared as though two of Emma's goats - because she supposed they *were* her goats - had hopped right over the slumped bit of fence and gone straight for the neighbor's garden.

What she couldn't figure out was how they had gotten out of their paddock to begin with. She briefly considered going over the same way that they had, but thought better of it. She was liable to injure herself climbing over that pile of bramble and wire, especially when she could hardly use her left hand.

She hurried around through the front gate and into the garden, where the neighbor lady was flapping a dish towel at the goats to no visible effect.

Emma grabbed the collar that the mother goat wore and tried pulling her away from the neighbor's cabbages, but the goat just planted her feet and gave her great rounded horns an irritated shake.

She tried grabbing the buckling, who was nearly as big as his mother, but he responded by butting her in the thigh. She thought that it was a playful headbutt, but she didn't really know them well enough to be sure. Playful or not, it was going to leave a bruise.

"Do you see?" the woman snapped. "What did I tell you about the fence?"

"I'm very sorry. I'll make sure it doesn't happen again."

"You can start by stopping it from happening right now!" She snapped a towel in the buckling's face, and he stepped away from her cabbage.

"Come on," Emma pleaded, taking the mother goat by one horn. "Come home."

The doe shook her off again, and Emma took a nervous step backwards as the buckling lowered his head.

"Feeding time!" Tara came through the gate with a bucket of feed, and the goats trotted right to her.

"Tell her to tie up those goats!" their neighbor shouted.

"Hello, Mrs. Rasmussen. Lovely day, isn't it?"

"Tara." Mrs. Rasmussen turned to Emma with a stony expression. "You owe me three heads of cabbage and... I'll have to survey the damage before I tell you the rest."

"Yes, well, I'll see to the fence, shall I?"

Mrs. Rasmussen harrumphed and stomped back into her house. Emma hurried to follow Tara and the goats back to her own front gate.

"Thank you so much," she said.

"I could hear her caterwauling from my place."

"You're a lifesaver."

"Anytime." Tara led the goats through the Kealoha front gate and handed the bucket to Emma. "After you get them back in their pen, you might want to come check on Kai."

"Is he okay?"

"I'm not sure. He was hunkered down in the fort for a while, looking grumpy."

"Okay, thanks. I'll be there in a minute."

Emma led the troublesome animals back to their paddock, which took up a generous portion of the back of the lot. She was horrified to find the gate open.

The other two goats were out as well, but they had opted to wreak havoc closer to home. Still, it was getting close to milking time, and they were happy enough to stop nibbling on the fruit trees and follow the green bucket back home.

She closed the gate behind her and gave the goats the small amount of grain that they were allowed as a treat.

It was there that she found Kai, hunkered down in the goat shed of all places. He was cuddling the fifth and final goat, an old wether that was too fat and lazy to have followed the others out of the open door. Or maybe he was just enjoying the attention.

"You left the gate open," she said, being careful to keep her tone neutral.

He just curled further into himself, pressing his cheek against the goat's side.

"When we leave the gate open, the goats can get out. Two of them went into the yard of the lady next door and started eating her garden."

"She has lots of goats in her yard," Kai said.

"Not Tara," she clarified. "The other neighbor. And they were nibbling on our fruit trees too. If they get out too often, they could eat everything up. The trees could die."

When he didn't reply, she crouched down nearby and tried to get a better look at his face. He refused to meet her eyes.

"What's wrong?"

"They didn't want to play with me."

"The twins?"

"Any of them."

"Oh, their friends?"

He nodded.

"It can be hard being the new kid on the block."

"It's not a block. It's a stupid jungle."

"Maybe if..." she started, but he stuck his fingers in his ears and squeezed his eyes shut.

She tried pulling one hand down, but he let out a low scream of frustration that scared away the placid fat goat he had been cuddling with.

"I hate it here!" He swatted her hand away and ran out the gate, leaving it wide open.

With a resigned sigh, she intercepted one of the goats before it got out again. Squeezing quickly through the gate and shutting it behind her, she went after Kai.

She found him in the bedroom where they had both slept the night before; he had been too frightened to sleep alone in the strange house. He was sitting in the corner of the room with a blanket over his head.

"Hey kiddo." She sat down close to him without touching his one-man fort.

"I didn't know where you were." He sounded close to tears.

"What?" When he didn't answer right away, she sat down next to him and waited out his silence.

"I came home and you weren't here. I couldn't find you."

"I was right here. I was just in the other room pulling cactus spines from my hand."

"Cactuses live in the desert."

"That's true. These were from the giant grass. The lady next door called it cactus grass. I'll show you what it looks like so you don't touch it by accident."

He was quiet for a while, sniffling beneath the blanket.

"Did you feel scared when you couldn't find me?" she asked gently.

"Yeah."

"Do you want a hug?"

He launched himself at her, pushed the blanket off of his head, and curled up in her lap. She rocked him gently, wiping the tears from his cheeks and kissing the top of his head.

"Maybe we should get some walkie talkies."

"What's that?"

"They're like phones that can only call each other. So if you're next door or if you're inside while I'm milking, you can always talk to me."

"Okay." He sighed. "I wish I could call Daddy."

Emma squeezed her eyes shut, swallowing back a sudden rush of tears.

"Me too, kiddo. Me too."

7

Lani

The first place on her list was north of Hilo, just above a little blip of a town called Pāpaʻikou.

The rental was farther from family than she wanted to be, but the rent was reasonable. It was the best deal that she had found in her hours scouring Craigslist and Facebook groups.

Lani turned left and drove up the old plantation road. It was narrow, with small houses crowded along both sides and newer houses up above. The ocean flashed blue and bright in her rearview mirror. In the back seat, Rory hummed along to kids' songs.

This property was way up at the top of the road, sitting on ten green acres of land with a view of the water. The century-old house had bright fresh paint. It looked idyllic surrounded by green sunshine and fruit trees. There was a trampoline back behind the orchard, level with the grass that grew up around it. She could hear the rush of a creek back behind the trees.

This was what she wanted for her daughter: a childhood full

of warm rain and sunshine, feasting on lychee right up in the tree.

She walked up the front steps and knocked on the door. There was a slight commotion inside and then a woman came out, closing the door quickly behind her. She gave Lani a harried smile that did nothing to hide her stress.

"Hey there! I'm Tammy. You must be Maria."

"No, I'm Lani. We spoke on the phone?"

"Yes, of course. Sorry, we have so many people interested in our private guest house." She let them around the wraparound porch, keeping up an incessant stream of chatter. "Really I think we priced it too low, but rent is just absurd here. I wouldn't feel good taking two thousand dollars for this little place like some people want, it's just not right. We got lucky, my mother-in-law bought this property ages ago, before things went so crazy. She's back on the mainland now, so here we are. Renting out the granny flat. It's actually where *we* lived, ironically. Well, that's before she was a granny anyhow. Then we outgrew it – we have four boys – and finally graduated to the main house. But the guest house has a place in my heart, it really does. Come on inside."

The place connected to the main porch, just behind the washer and dryer. Its front door was directly across from the back door of the main house, just a few feet away. She caught a glimpse of four boys sitting at the kitchen table, their father standing over them.

"We homeschool," Tammy said. "Though sometimes I'm not sure why. It's a fight to get them to do the littlest thing."

She glanced through the window again at the four boys stuck inside on such a glorious day. But she shouldn't judge. Living here, they probably spent nearly their whole lives running free, catching tadpoles in the creek. She turned back to her potential landlady.

"That's what I'm planning to do with Rory. My cousin runs a co-op, lots of outdoor play and hands-on learning."

"Oh, a co-op would be nice. We tried one up in Waimea, but it just didn't click. Here's that key! Come on through."

It was an odd layout, a long rectangle that went from living room to walk-in closet to bathroom to kitchen to bedroom. But the living room and bedroom each had big glass doors that looked out on overgrown grass and blue sky, nothing in sight but nature. The kitchen window was the same.

"It's so beautiful up here," Lani said, watching a saffron finch land sideways on a stalk of cane grass.

"I like it!" Rory climbed up onto the queen-sized bed that took up most of the tiny bedroom. When she stood, she could look over the wall and into the kitchen.

A day gecko peered down at her from the rafters. Its bright green head was spotted with orange, and its huge black eyes were rimmed with sky blue. Rory squealed and clapped her hands together in delight, and the gecko disappeared.

"You take your time and look around," Tammy said. "I need to get the laundry in before the weather changes."

Lani looked around carefully. The kitchen was small but workable. The whole place was. And they wouldn't spend much time inside anyhow, in a place this beautiful.

"Is this our new house?" Rory asked.

"Maybe. Let's go talk to the lady."

As they walked back out onto the shared porch, a little boy pushed through the screen door. He was just a bit older than Rory, probably five years old.

"Hi!" Rory said brightly. "What's your name?"

"Billy. Want to catch lizards?"

"Okay!"

They inched down the steps, stalking a bright green anole lizard. It flashed the red dewlap on its neck in and out like a folding fan. Just as Billy got close enough to catch it, his father burst through the screen door and grabbed him by the back of his shirt. Lani flinched and stepped backwards, startled.

"Where do you think you're going?" the man shouted.

Rory ran to hide behind her mama's legs.

"Stop!" Billy fought like a wild thing, slapping and scraping at his father's arm as he was dragged backwards into the house. "Stop it!"

"Four lines! It's not hard! Are you stupid? Or just lazy?"

Lani stood frozen in place as the screen door slammed shut behind them. Her heart was racing, cortisol pumping through her veins. After the past couple of years with Zeke, it didn't take much for her body to go into full flight or freeze.

"I am so sorry about that!" Tammy's voice was overbright as she hurried up the porch steps. "Those boys just do not listen. All I wanted was one nice, quiet little girl. Like this one here." She grinned at Rory, who whimpered.

"Thanks very much for your time," Lani said quickly. She swung Rory up onto her hip and hurried down the front steps.

"Did you want to put down a deposit?" Tammy called after her. "There are other folks interested!"

"No thanks!" Lani yanked the car door open. "We've got a few other places to look at today."

"Alright." She deflated, her voice suddenly tired. "Well, you let me know."

She went back into the house, and the clang of the screen door made Lani wince.

How long until her nervous system settled back into some semblance of normalcy?

"Get in the car, baby."

Rory released her vice grip with some reluctance and crawled into the back seat.

Inside, Tammy cursed at her husband. "I told you someone was coming to see the guest house today!"

"And I told you I don't want anyone living right on my ass!" he shouted back.

Lani's hands shook as she clipped Rory into her car seat.

"Mama," Rory whispered urgently, "I don't want to live here."

"Me neither, baby. Let's see what else we can find."

The first place that they visited in Hilo reeked of black mold and ammonia. The second turned them away as soon as they saw Rory, even though Lani had *said* in her email that she was a single mother. The third, a room in someone's house, informed her that both the kitchen and the living room were off limits.

Things didn't get any better as they worked their way south.

One listing that had shown only a picture of the beautiful yard turned out to have no house at all. The five hundred dollars per month that they were asking for was simply to set up a tent or park a van on the empty lot.

They visited a cute farm shack, and the setting was idyllic... then Lani realized that the shack was attached to the farm's mac nut processor, which would make an unbearable racket on the regular.

"Can we go home now?" Rory whined as they drove away from the mac nut farm.

Where's home? Lani wondered.

"Just one more stop," she said aloud. "Do you want some more of that dried mango?"

The last place on her list was a reasonably priced rental south of Pualena. The satellite navigation led her off of the pavement and onto a dirt road that became gradually more pitted the farther she drove, until it could hardly be called a road anymore. It became a series of steep hills and valleys that threatened to strand them. She could just see them out there, miles from the highway, no cell service, tires spinning in the air.

She drove so slowly that the appointment time came and went with her still a few miles away, staring down a pond-sized puddle that took up the entire road.

She called the contact number for the rental and waited.

"Hello?" said a gruff voice.

"Hi, this is Lani, I was supposed to come see your rental at two. I'm almost there, but the road is flooded. Is there another way around?"

"No way around, it's a dead end."

"I'm scared I'm gonna wreck my cousin's car."

"It's not as bad as it looks. Just stay to the right."

She eyed the puddle for another moment, but she couldn't do it. Not in 'Ōlena's minivan. Anyway, how would she even get out here? She needed her own car. She was going about this whole thing backwards.

"Could I come back next week?"

"It'll be rented by then." The guy hung up.

"Can we go home now?" Rory asked again, drawing the words out into a whine.

"Yeah, baby." Lani made a ten-point turn on the narrow dirt road and went back the way they had come, driving carefully around the ridges and valleys. "Let's go home."

She drove the short distance to Pualena and pulled up to her aunt's house, feeling exhausted.

"Any luck?" 'Ōlena asked as they walked in.

"Nope." Lani handed her keys back and joined her at the kitchen table as Rory ran off in search of her cousins. "Thanks for letting me use your van."

"Finding a place to live here is no joke. Why you think I still live with my parents?"

"I would love to live with my parents," she said, her voice barely audible.

"Leilani." 'Ōlena reached out and took her hand. "I'm sorry. I shouldn't—"

"No, it's okay." She stood and went to fill the kettle. "Do you want some tea?"

"There's no rush. My mom loves having you here."

"I know." She set the kettle over a flame and put a few red-veined *māmaki* leaves in her aunt's old teapot. "And I'm grateful, I am. I just... you know I've never had a place of my own?"

"Never?"

She shook her head and crossed her arms, leaning back against the kitchen counter. "I went from my parent's house to the dorms to cruise ships to Zeke's place."

"And now you're sleeping in the office, with my dad knocking at six in the morning because he wants to print something."

She chuckled ruefully. "Yep."

"That's rough."

"But it was stupid to go look at rentals when I don't even have a car. I need to figure that out first."

"Figure what out?" Kekoa asked, coming through to the fridge.

"What you doing here?" his sister scolded. "You have your own kitchen."

"There's no food in my kitchen."

"And whose fault is that?"

"I been busy with work." He pulled out the leftover laulau that his mom and grandmother had made.

"No wonder your kid is always over here at dinnertime."

He rolled his eyes and turned to Lani. "What you need to figure out?"

"I need a car." She filled the teapot and set the lid on to let it steep.

"What's your budget?"

She ran through the numbers in her head, thinking over the last of the savings she had left from her cruise ship days, the shares of mutual funds that she could sell. So much for her meager retirement fund. She still needed to hold at least half of that back for first, last, and deposit on a rental, so... "Three thousand? Maybe four?"

"Anything you buy for three thousand gonna be a lemon."

She slumped, exhausted.

"Don't worry. We'll find you something. Fix it up. Just don't buy nothing without me or Dad having a look at it."

"Okay. Thanks, Kekoa."

"You'll get back on your feet," 'Ōlena said. "It just takes time."

Kekoa grinned. "And you on island time now."

8

Emma

Emma had just sat down with a cup of coffee when her new walkie talkie clicked and crackled. Kai's sleepy voice came through asking, "Where are you?"

"I'm right outside on the *lanai*. Come have a cuddle."

Kai came stumbling out a moment later wearing a fuzzy blanket like a cloak. He rubbed his eyes and curled up next to her on the bench.

As Emma put an arm around him, she felt a rare moment of peace.

The world was alive with birdsong. Bright yellow saffron finches gathered by the dozens, hopping across the lawn in search of miniscule bugs and seeds. Roosters crowed all around the neighborhood, reminding competitors that this was *their* patch of earth and their harem.

Everywhere she looked, the rain-damp plants shone vibrant colors. Coleus plants surged all around the lanai, pushing out ruffled leaves of bright magenta trimmed with lime green. They were still wet from the rain that fell nearly every night.

The water beaded on their leaves sparkled in the first golden light of morning.

She had been up for hours already. There was fresh goat's milk in the fridge, and all of the animals had fresh water. This stillness felt well deserved, radically different from the heavy depression of the past few months.

There were a thousand things that she couldn't even think about yet. The overgrown orchard, crumbling outbuildings, fences collapsing under the weight of weeds and vines. This place needed so much more than she had to give.

But if she pushed all that to the far back of her mind and just gave herself over to the demands of the day, there was a deep peace to be found in the rhythm of farm chores. Feeding the animals, milking the goats morning and night, slowly cleaning out the farmhouse... it all gave her a feeling of purpose that was its own kind of medicine. The to-do list that came with this hobby farm was never ending, and Emma had given herself over to it.

Back home in Redwood Grove with nothing to do, with a house that basically took care of itself and a fridge full of sympathy meals, she had sunk into a numbness that bordered on death. Here, she had a reason to get up in the morning – quite literally, things that she *had* to get up and do or else other living beings would suffer.

Best of all, Kai was coming alive again too. She felt immense guilt that caring for her son hadn't been enough to pull her out of her deep depression, but they had been stuck in the same hole. And then Hawai'i had lowered down a sturdy vine and made it possible for them to climb out.

They were still climbing. But that in itself was something.

Beside her, Kai stirred.

"What's for breakfast?" he asked sleepily.

"French toast?" she suggested.

"Okay," he yawned.

"Ready for an egg hunt?"

He sat up all the way. "Yeah!"

"Okay. You go round up some eggs, and I'll pick oranges for juice."

"Ready, go!" He jumped up and raced off, already familiar with the hens' favorite spots.

Emma walked barefoot across the wet lawn to an orange tree that was heavy with fruit. They were still mostly green, but she had learned that the oranges here rarely turned orange, at least on the outside. Something to do with the temperatures never dipping low enough to trigger a change. Inside, though, they were as sweet and juicy as anything.

Kai was already in the kitchen when she got back.

And so was Myrtle.

"Kai, no. I told you, no chickens in the house."

"But Mom!" He scooped the fluffy gray chicken up off of the floor. "I *had* to let her in. One of the roosters kept jumping on her."

She passed a hand over her eyes. "Be that as it may, she belongs outside."

"You're so mean!" Kai stomped his foot, and Myrtle squirmed in his arms.

Emma opened the kitchen door, and he carried Myrtle outside. She tried to run right back in, but Emma blocked her and steered her back out with a gentle foot.

"Go on. Go find some nice juicy worms." She closed the door, and Kai glared up at her. "What?"

He stomped back to the kitchen table and started candling

the eggs that he'd collected. It wasn't really necessary, since he collected fresh eggs from the same spots each day, but he loved passing each egg over the flashlight. And ever since the twins had shown him a half-developed egg, he had to make sure that there were no babies in the pastel rainbow of chicken eggs that he gathered each day.

She walked over and rubbed his back. "Ready for French toast?"

"I guess."

"Do you want to help me?"

"Okay." He looked up at her, grumpiness receding. "You break them, and I'll stir."

"Deal."

They set about making breakfast together the way that they had so many times before, and a priceless sense of contentment filled her chest.

The grief was still there – and fear too, that this delicate return to normalcy might not last – but those feelings were quieter now. Manageable.

"Myrtle lays blue eyes," Kai told her as he ate his French toast.

"Oh yeah?"

"Yeah."

"How do you know?"

"She has her own secret spot."

Her phone dinged with a text and she picked it up, expecting something from one of her sisters. They both checked in daily, outwardly cheerful but really just terrified about how she was faring out in the middle of the ocean when she had barely been functioning at home.

Instead, she found a text from Lani: *What are you up to today?*

No plans, Emma replied. *Other than a grocery run, we haven't even left the neighborhood since we got here last week.*

Up for a beach day? I know a great spot for the kids with no crowds. But I need a ride.

A beach day sounds great. Drop me a pin.

She picked up Kai's breakfast plate and put it in the sink.

"Can I watch YouTube?" he asked.

"Not right now, hon. We're going to get ready for the beach."

His little face pulled into a frown. "I don't want to go to the beach."

"We're going to pick up Auntie Lani and your cousin Rory, remember them? They're going to show us a new–"

"I don't want to go to the stupid beach!" he shouted.

Emma stilled. This had been their pattern back in California, ever since losing Adam. Any time she tried to get Kai out the door, he would lose it. Sometimes she would lose it right back. Mostly, though, she just wilted and gave in. Getting him over whatever inner hurdle was causing those overblown reactions took more energy than she had.

Not today.

She moved closer and got down to his level. "Our cousins don't have a car yet, and they asked for a ride. Going to the beach is really good for our bodies, including our hearts and our brains. And I already told them that we would go. Would you please put your bathing suit on?"

He crossed his arms. "Can I watch YouTube after?"

A *No* rose in her throat, but she gritted her teeth against it. There was a bright flash of childhood memory, her mother screaming at them on a sunny summer day.

"I'm going to throw that TV through the f-ing wall!"

She took a deep breath.

"Sure. We can watch for half an hour when we get home."

"Two hours," he countered.

Emma bit back a laugh. "Zero hours."

"Fine," he said in a long-suffering tone. "Half an hour."

"Bathing suit."

He walked away, dragging his feet. Emma's shoulders fell in relief. Meltdown averted.

Multiple times a day, she wondered if they should just go cold turkey on the screens. But back in the before times, screens had only added to their lives. They used to use games and videos as jumping off points for their homeschool lessons. An episode on moles led to a stack of library books on those underground explorers. When he was obsessed with *Number Blocks* at age five, Emma had made paper dolls of each number-based character and Kai would stack them on top of each other at the kitchen table.

"Seven plus three equals ten!"

That show had even taught him square numbers, a concept that he mimicked and explored with blocks on the floor: *"The square root of sixteen is four!"* Things that she never would have thought to introduce so early, rendered easy and fun through cartoons and songs.

Screens weren't inherently bad. And yanking his primary coping mechanism out from under him all at once wasn't the answer either.

Connection over control.

It was her mantra, the running theme of all of the books on parenting and child development that filled her shelves back home. She knew what her son needed.

She had just been sunk too deep in grief to give him that.

But that was a blip. An inevitable interlude. She could get

back to her best self again.

She had to.

"Thank you so much for picking us up," Lani gushed as she wrestled her daughter's car seat into the back of Emma's car.

"Thanks for the invitation," Emma replied. "We needed to get out. There's so much to do on the property that it's easy to go all week without going anywhere at all, but it's a shame not to get to the beach while we're here."

"Are you ready for a beach day, Kai?"

He turned away from her and scowled out the window, arms crossed tight over his chest in a posture that screamed, *Don't talk to me!*

Emma gave Lani an apologetic look, which she dismissed with a shrug and a smile. Car seat secured, she scooted back out of the car and smiled at her daughter.

"Ready, Freddy?"

She giggled. "My name's Rory!"

"That's right! Silly me. Hop on in."

Once they were cruising up the highway towards Hilo, Lani put a hand over hers and asked, "How are you holding up, really?"

"I'm doing okay. Sunshine and sweat are good medicine. I'm closer to normal than I've been in a long time."

"That's great, Em."

"Getting away from the constant reminders helped, I think. I mean, they're here too. Pictures of Adam when he was Kai's age. All the summers we spent here when we were young. But it's not the same as being in our house every day without him. It helps me feel closer to him, being here. Instead of just feeling the hole where he should be."

"That makes sense."

"How are you doing?"

"I don't even know." Lani laughed, but the sound was all stress. She looked over her shoulder at Rory, who was rocking out to the *Moana* songs that were blasting on the back speakers. She turned back to Emma and said, "Getting here was this huge rush, you know? Getting out with my girl, making it home. It was this heady feeling of freedom."

"And now?"

"Now it's all catching up with me. The rental market here is insane. I'm working at Kekoa's shave ice place, and I'm so grateful to have a job and childcare, but it still doesn't come anywhere close to covering what rent costs here. Anything in my price range is horrific. Tiny rooms with peeling wallpaper I could handle, but not the black mold.

"And then car prices are just as bad, so I don't know how I would move out even if I did find a place. So it's just me and Rory on an airbed in Manō's office. And we're lucky to even have that, but it's not sustainable."

"Come stay with us," Emma said.

She didn't need to think it over. She knew in her gut that Lani moving in would be the best possible thing for everybody. What's more, it's exactly what Adam would have said. And he would have said it sooner, as soon as he heard that she was back.

Lani was shaking her head. "You don't have to do that."

"We have so much space."

She shifted uncomfortably. "I wasn't hinting at anything."

"I know you weren't. But the space is there, okay? Think about it. You can have John's truck."

Her jaw dropped. "Are you serious?"

"I don't need it. It's just sitting there. It's technically Kai's, but come on. We've got another decade before he can drive."

"You're serious."

"Lani, I don't know what I'm going to do with that place. I can't leave the house to rot and give the whole lot back to the jungle, but I can't stay here forever either."

"Why not?"

"We have a life in California. Or we used to." Emma shook her head quickly, steeling herself. "My whole family's there. My brother's wife is about to have a baby. I can't stay here forever."

"How long are you here?"

"A while," Emma said with a shrug. She wasn't ready to grapple with that question. "It's been good for us so far, and there's a lot to figure out. If you want your own room while you get back on your feet, well. It's there."

"I might take you up on that."

"So where do I turn?" she asked as they neared the coastline.

"Just go right up there, and then follow the road all the way to the end."

They parked in a dirt lot at the end of the road, and from there it was a short and glorious hike to the secret beach. Kai fell in love with the place immediately, racing off across the black rock and spring-green grass that grew year round.

The ponds and streams that they crossed were cold, fed by freshwater springs that came up just a few yards back from the ocean. The water was crystal clear. Even in the deepest parts, they could see to the bottom with astonishing clarity. Tiny silver fish darted around a fallen log, scales glinting in the sun as they turned.

They set up camp for the day on a miniscule sandy beach

sheltered by high rocks on either side. It faced a clear, calm lagoon where the kids could play endlessly without their parents standing over them. Trees towered all around, scraggly pines that grew straight out of the lava rock. They made her think of redwoods – tall and thin and tough as hell.

"What are these trees called, do you know?"

"Ironwood," Lani supplied. She lay on her back on a towel, watching the slender branches sway overhead.

"Are they pine trees?" Dry brown needles carpeted the lava rock. They were similar to pine needles, but more delicate, scaled and segmented into pieces that came apart instead of bending the way that pine needles did.

"Not related. They're from Australia." Lani picked up one of the thin needles and broke it methodically into segments. "My biology teacher in high school used them as an example of convergent evolution. She was the best."

"How do they grow right on top of the rocks like that?"

"They're nitrogen fixers."

"What does that mean?"

"Basically it means that they eat the air."

"That's crazy." Emma looked up at the lacy pattern that the needles made against the clear blue sky. "Coastal redwoods can survive without rain. They get all of the water they need from the fog. But growing without soil, in a place that they didn't even evolve in... that's something else."

"Life finds a way." Lani sat up and looked at her. "Are you sure? About us moving in?"

Emma nodded. "It's too much for me. I'd be grateful for the help."

"I can pay rent."

"Please don't."

"I can—"

"No," Emma interrupted her. A fierce grief rose in her chest, but she pushed through it. "I have Adam's life insurance. I have *more* money coming that the government gives to the families of firefighters who—" She swallowed and shook her head. "We have the house, the truck. It's more than we need. More than I even want. It feels so weird to take on the responsibility for Kealoha land, even if I'm just stewarding it for my son. And you're family. Please come stay with us. Stay as long as you'd like."

Lani's eyes shone with tears. She took Emma's hand in a crushing grip. "Thank you."

Emma leaned closer and hugged her. "Thank *you*."

9

Lani

The rain was spitting that morning, little needles blowing sideways, and Rory refused to get out of the car. She huddled under a beach towel and shivered dramatically.

"I can't go. It's too cold."

"Aurora King, you were born in Alaska. This drizzle is not *cold*."

"It's freezing." Rory chattered her teeth together, and Lani laughed.

"That's pretty good."

"We can't swim in the rain."

"You don't have to. It'll be sunny in a couple of hours. You can swim then."

"I want to go home."

"Not an option." She scooped her up and out of the car.

"It's like you're torturing me!" Rory went limp, letting her head loll back. The misting rain landed on her pale cheeks and dark hair, a thousand miniscule droplets.

"We should get you into a theater troupe."

She perked up. "What's that?"

"Plays."

"Playing?"

"Acting. Pretending. Like in movies."

"I like movies!"

"I know." Lani set her down at the edge of the parking lot and adjusted the beach bag she had slung over one shoulder.

"Lani!" Emma rolled down the driver-side window of her car as she pulled up. "Hi! 'Ōlena said you would be here. Where does her group meet up?"

"On the grass usually, but they're over there today." She pointed to a blue structure just past the parking lot, four columns and a roof. "See the picnic tables?"

"Great, thanks. I'll just park up here."

"Look," she told Rory. "Auntie 'Ōlena is setting up out of the rain. Run and catch up with your cousins."

Rory ran off towards the big girls, and Lani walked over to Emma. She gave her a hug when she got out of the car.

"How's it going?"

"I spent most of my morning trying to coax a goat back through a gate. Would not follow me. Would not budge when I pulled on her collar. Finally the two little girls next door did it for me. They called to her and she went right in."

"Thank God for neighbors."

"We've got good ones."

"So I told my auntie that we'll be staying with you a while. I can be ready tomorrow, if you don't mind picking me up."

"Yeah, tomorrow's fine."

"Are you starting Kai in the co-op?"

"No, I don't think so. Getting him down here today was hard

enough. But I want him to have more time with his cousins. Are you staying?"

"For a little while. I have work later."

Emma opened the back door of her car. "Come on, come see your cousins."

"No!" Kai pulled the door closed again, but Emma caught it.

"Kai, please. It'll be fun."

"No! I hate it here!" He wrenched the door shut.

"We had a similar morning," Lani said. "Rory used to bound out into the snow like a husky, but a bit of warm rain in Hawai'i and suddenly she's the wicked witch."

"What?"

"I'm melting!" Lani croaked, lifting her arms to shield herself from the mist that hung in the air. Emma laughed and shook her head. Lani straightened up and asked, "Is he having a hard time adjusting to life in a new place?"

"He's having a hard time adjusting to life without his dad," she said in a low voice. Lani put a sympathetic hand on her arm as she continued, "It was even worse in California. He's been doing better here. We both have. He's happy enough when we're home – at John's place, I mean. He adores the little girls who live next door. But if I try to get him to do something that he doesn't want to do, it's just a nightmare. Especially getting in the car and going anywhere. I don't know why it's so hard."

"It's normal."

Emma slumped against the back of her car. "My mom keeps sending me articles on oppositional defiant disorder and treatment plans."

"Yikes."

"Yeah. She thinks she's being helpful. She's not."

"He'll come around, Em. It takes time."

She frowned, looking over her shoulder. "Whose dog is that?"

Lani turned to see a puppy slinking closer. He was half grown, maybe six months old. Beautiful, like a German Shepherd but sleeker... and so skinny she could see his ribs. He crouched down in a submissive posture, tail wagging nervously.

"Emma, you came!" 'Ōlena walked up and hugged her, then turned to Lani. "Do you have the baking soda and vinegar?"

"No. Are they still in the car?"

"Must be."

"Hey, do you know whose dog this is?"

She frowned at the puppy, who was still hovering nearby. "Someone dumped him a couple months ago. Lady who lives nearby feeds him, but she can't get close enough to grab him."

"He's skinny," Emma murmured.

"He's got worms, probably. Lani, will you give me a hand with the science stuff?"

"Sure."

As they walked away, she heard Emma's car door open behind her.

"Kai, are you going to eat that quesadilla?"

"No!"

"Do you want to toss it to this puppy?"

Lani looked over her shoulder and saw Kai climbing out of the car. The puppy crept closer, tail wagging in a blur, but he was too scared to take the food out of Kai's hand.

She helped 'Ōlena set up the day's science experiment slash art project. There was a baking sheet for each kid, plus watercolor paper and vinegar that they mixed with dye. By the time everything was set up, the clouds had burned off and the kids were splashing in the lagoon.

"Want me to round them up?" Lani asked.

"No rush," 'Ōlena said. "We can do it after lunch."

"Okay. I should head out soon. I'm just going to say goodbye to Rory."

Her daughter was playing happily with her cousins, but she ran over as soon as she saw Lani split off from the other moms.

"I want a snack!"

"Auntie 'Ōlena has the snacks." Lani crouched down and opened her arms for a hug. "I need to head to work soon."

"I won't let you go." Rory put her head under the hem of Lani's t-shirt, trying to crawl in there with her.

"You have so much fun with Auntie 'Ōlena and your cousins," Lani coaxed. She fixed her shirt and pulled Rory into her arms.

"Only when you're there."

"Baby, I have to go to work."

"I can go to work with you. I'm a good helper."

"You are. You're such a good helper. But I have to do this by myself."

"No. I won't let you."

"You're doing a science experiment today."

Rory curled more tightly into her. "I hate science."

"That's a strong word," Lani told her.

"I don't care. I'm not letting you leave."

Lani sighed and sat down on a cold concrete bench, holding Rory on her lap. She was getting taller by the minute, a bundle of limbs. So big and still so little.

She couldn't have asked for a more idyllic childcare situation, but leaving her here was still so hard. Being away from her at all went against her every instinct, and trying to reassure her through that felt impossible. She was sure that Rory could feel her anxiety, and that just made it worse.

"I can stay for ten more minutes, but then I really need to go. And tomorrow I'm staying all day, remember? We'll all make a big, big chalk art together."

Rory sniffed. "Can we make a rainbow?"

"Definitely we can make a rainbow." Lani looked up and saw Lulu's golden-haired friend running down from the parking lot. "Look, here comes Olivia."

"Who?"

"She gave you the flower, remember? For painting?"

"Oh yeah." She sat up a bit straighter, allowing a bare inch of air to come between her and her mother. "She's really nice."

"She *is* nice."

"Hi Olivia!"

"Hi Rory! Look at my shoes!" Olivia jumped, and the sides of the soles flashed rainbow colors.

"Woah!"

"Are you okay?" She frowned in concern at the younger girl's tear-streaked face, and Lani wiped her cheeks.

"I'm okay!" Rory wriggled away from her mom to stand in front of Olivia. "We're doing science today!"

"What kind of science?"

"I don't know."

"Let's go ask!" Olivia took Rory's hand and ran to 'Ōlena. Lani watched them with a smile, anxiety slowly releasing its vice grip on her heart.

They had been so isolated in Alaska. Just the two of them, day after day. And she had loved it, that part of it. Being with her baby all the time. But this was healthy. This was what she wanted for her.

"Lani King." The male voice made her jump, and her hands flew up in surprise. But it was just Alfie – *Tenn*, she corrected herself. His hair was down today, thick dark waves that stopped just short of his shoulders. His glass-brown eyes met hers, and a thrum of awareness ran through her.

"Alfred Lord Tennyson," she said.

"I know I said you could call me anything," he said lightly, "but it feels like you're abusing the privilege."

"Sorry," she laughed. "Tenn."

"Better." He held her eyes long enough that she blushed and looked away, out over the calm water of the lagoon. "What are you up to?"

"Just dropping my daughter off with her cousins." Her fingers pressed against the rough concrete as she waited for this cute younger guy to lose all interest at the first mention of a kid. Instead he leaned forward, trying to look her in the eye again.

"How old is your daughter?"

"Four. Almost five."

"Livie's six."

Lani's spine straightened as she turned to face him. "Olivia?"

"Yeah, she—"

"Daddy!" The little blond girl ran over to stand in front of Tenn. "Where's my water?"

He handed over a canvas bag and she was off again, back to the group.

"You have a daughter?" Lani asked in amazement. "That's your daughter?"

"That's her." He smiled softly, watching her run off. Then he took in the surprise on Lani's face and shrugged. "She looks like her mom. And *my* mom, really. Livie resembles her more than anyone."

"She— so her—" Lani stumbled over her words, not wanting

to ask outright if he was single.

"Her mom died last year," he said quietly.

"Oh, Tenn. I'm so sorry."

"No, it's okay. I mean, not *okay*, it's my kid's mom. But we weren't together." He ran a hand through his hair, frowning. "She was barely around even before she died. We coparented from the beginning, but by the time Livie was three, her mom just took her the occasional weekend. So it wasn't as hard as it could have been. Not that there's anything worse than seeing my daughter hurt, but I was solid. I was able to be there for her in a way that I wouldn't have if I had been grieving that same way, you know?"

"Yeah."

"My parents help out a lot. And 'Ōlena. This program was a Godsend. Livie's been in it since the start, about two years now. But yeah, mostly it's just the two of us." He joined her on the bench. "I'm not seeing anyone."

A jolt of fear went through her, and she looked away. It didn't matter. It didn't matter how cute he was, or how sweet his daughter was. She was nowhere near ready for another relationship. She wasn't even out of the last one, not legally.

Rory ran up to stand in front of her mom, hands on her hips. "Are you still here?"

Lani laughed, and her fear drained away. *Look where you are,* she thought to herself. *Blue skies and sunshine and a perfect little girl. There's nothing to be scared of here.*

"I'm still here," she confirmed.

"Is it ten minutes yet?"

"Almost."

"You're gonna be late for work!"

"Okay, okay, I'm going!" She stood, and Rory launched

herself into a hug that just about knocked her over. Then she was off again, shouting at her cousins.

"Can I give you a ride to town?" Tenn asked.

She opened her mouth to say no, but nothing came out. All through college and her cruise ship years, she was perfectly at ease around guy friends. But five years with Zeke had eroded that confidence. She didn't feel safe or comfortable around men anymore.

Her uncle and cousin were the exception, men she had known all her life. But she found that these days, being around any man she didn't know well put her hackles up. She hated this part of herself, this new defensive fear, but she didn't have any idea of how to uproot it. Strange men made her nervous.

But this was *Alfie*. Alfred Nakamura with his green and purple pens. The sweet boy who had kept her from failing precalc. He had been the soul of kindness then, and her gut told her that was still true. She made a mental note to ask 'Ōlena about him.

"I'm headed to the restaurant," he told her, "and I'll be back later to pick up Livie. You can ride with me if you want to. No pressure."

"Yeah." She took a breath. "Okay. Thanks."

He smiled, and her stomach did a little somersault. "Anytime, Lani King."

10

Emma

All of the kids in 'Ōlena's co-op were sweet and inclusive, but Kai still hovered on the edge of things. Emma hung back, hoping that he would join in the fun with his cousins and their friends. No such luck. He steered clear of them all morning, paying more attention to the stray pup than the other kids.

Even the baking soda and vinegar only held him close to the group for a few minutes. It was a brilliant activity, science meets art, but Kai wasn't impressed. He went along with it in a halfhearted way and then wandered off again.

Adam would have known how to help him through this.

It was an absurd thing to think, when it was his death that had caused this crippling grief in the first place. Still, she couldn't help but think it. If the tables were turned, if she were the one who was gone, Adam would be doing better by their son than she had so far. He would have done a better job at keeping him engaged with the land of the living.

Help me, she pleaded, looking at a tiny cloud that moved

across the ocean, miles away. *Help me know how to help him.*

She was still staring out at the ocean, lost in thought, when Kai walked up.

"Do we have food?" he asked.

"Are you hungry?"

"What do we have?"

"Let's see." She looked through the bag she had thrown together. "We've got a bunch of mandarin oranges, some celery and peanut butter, beef jerky–"

"Beef jerky," he said quickly. Then, as an afterthought, "And peanut butter."

She handed them over. "I think your cousins are going to have lunch soon if you want to sit with them."

"No thanks." He ran off towards the edge of the beach park and sat down in the shade, his back to a tree – and the other kids. Emma sighed and looked back out at the ocean.

A call came in from her little sister, and she picked up.

"Emma! You actually answered!"

"I'm not that bad."

"Yeah, okay." She could practically hear Liz rolling her eyes. "You occasionally reply to our texts, and we appreciate that proof of life, but we haven't had an actual phone call since you left."

"It's been a bit of a whirlwind, but we're starting to settle in."

"Don't get too settled. We miss you."

Emma braced herself for a wave of homesickness. But in that moment, looking out over Hilo Bay, she felt... nothing. Home had stopped feeling like home when Adam died. There, his absence was a black hole that swallowed everything else. Here, her grief wasn't such a hungry void.

"Emma? Are you there?"

"Yeah, I'm here."

"When are you coming home?"

"I'm not sure. I have to find new homes for all of the animals. Or a tenant who wants to take all of that on. Either way, it's going to take a while."

"Have you posted ads?"

"Not yet."

"You can't hide out in Hawai'i forever."

"I'm not hiding," she snapped. Then she sighed. "How are you? How are the girls?"

She listened to her sister talk about life in the mountains, but she didn't have her full attention. Her focus drifted to the green-hulled beach almonds that lay scattered across the springy grass, the gentle crash of waves against the far-off rocks that bordered the lagoon, the faint rainbow that followed the showers that fell out over the sea.

She looked over her shoulder to check on her son.

Back behind the picnic area, Kai was laying down a trail of beef jerky.

Four hours later, he was still there.

He had spent the whole day with the puppy. His cousins and their friends had donated bits and pieces of their lunches to the cause, and he patiently fed the dog tidbits for hours. Towards the end of the day, when the other parents were coming to pick up their kids, Emma went over and crouched beside Kai.

"It's time to head home, kiddo."

"Okay. How do we get him in the car?"

Emma looked over at the dog. He slunk a bit further away, head and tail held low.

"Honey, I don't think we can."

"We can't just leave him." He looked at her with huge, hurt eyes. "He needs us."

This close, Emma could see that the dog had an open wound on one of his legs. It cut deep, and the paw below it looked hurt and swollen as well. A car drove past and he ran towards the jungle, favoring his injured paw. She sighed and straightened up again.

"I'll see what I can do."

Lani was back from work. She stood talking to ʻŌlena with Rory clinging to her like a monkey.

"Hey," Emma said as she walked up, "do you know of any shelters nearby? Ideally one that would come get the dog?"

"You can call animal control," ʻŌlena told her, "but they'll just put him down."

Rory's head popped up from her mother's shoulder. "Put him down where?"

"He's just a puppy," Emma protested.

ʻŌlena nodded, her face sad as she looked across the lot. The dog wouldn't let anyone else within eight feet of him, but Kai was scratching him behind his ears.

"He's a big puppy, and the shelters are full. You can try one of the private rescues, but they're even more overwhelmed."

"Is Holoholona still around?" Lani asked.

"Might be." ʻŌlena's attention pulled to the side and she walked away, shouting, "Luana! Do not throw things at your sister! You want her to fall out of that tree?"

"Here." Lani showed Emma a page she'd pulled up on her phone, *Holoholona Rescue*. "There's a phone number."

"Thanks."

"Hello?" A woman picked up on the first ring.

"Hi there, is this Holoholona Rescue?"

"Yes, this is Kathy." Her voice was tired but kind. "How can I help you?"

"We found a puppy at Keiki Beach, and I'm wondering what can be done for him."

"The Belgian Malinois?"

"Um, he looks like some kind of Shepherd mix? About six months old?"

"More like eight or ten, I think. But he's underfed, maybe the runt. And he definitely has parasites. People have been calling about him for a few weeks, ever since he got dumped. Some breeder who couldn't sell the whole litter probably dumped him there. We've gone out a few times, but he's too skittish to catch."

"My son is petting him right now."

"Wow. That's better than we've managed. Do you think you can get him to the vet?"

"I don't know if I can get him in the car. If I can, do you have room at your shelter?"

Kathy gave a tired, one-note laugh. "Honey, my 'shelter' is a one-bedroom house with a pocket-sized yard. I have fourteen dogs here right now. We've got a good number of foster homes, but every one of them has more animals than they should. Same as every rescue on the island."

Emotion pressed against the back of Emma's throat as she watched the tired puppy lay his head in Kai's lap.

"Just don't call animal control," Kathy said.

"Okay."

"I'll ask around and see if I can find a foster. Get him in the car if you can. I know a vet who can see him last minute. I'll text you the address."

"Okay, thanks."

"Thank you for caring."

The call disconnected, and she looked at Lani.

"You think we can get them in the car?"

"I think Kai can."

She was right. With the help of a spam musubi from a discarded lunch bag, the puppy followed Kai right into the back seat. He shrank with fear when Emma closed the door behind him.

She leaned against the car and put a hand over her eyes, suddenly very tired. She could hear her mother's voice in her head.

You're supposed to be selling animals off, not taking more home.

But it was all that she could do to stand her ground when Kai fought her on things that were in his best interest, like getting off of screens and out into the world. She couldn't fight him on this, not when his heart was in the right place.

She walked around to the driver's side and got in. The puppy had his whole face burrowed behind Kai's back. But Kai was smiling, and that was enough for her.

"Hey Kai, do you know what fostering is?"

Kai was petting the frightened dog and murmuring reassurances. He looked up at her and shook his head.

"It means we help the puppy heal and get used to being around people, and then we find him a forever home. Are you up for that?"

"Yeah!"

"Okay. Let's get this guy to the vet."

Fostering was a good plan. A solid compromise. But as she drove slowly through the parking lot, glancing at Kai in the rearview mirror, she knew in her gut that this wasn't going to be a temporary thing.

Their flight home, whenever it happened, would be carrying one frightened dog in the cargo hold.

11

Lani

"Whatchoo doin?" Rory asked in a singsong, climbing up into her lap. Lani sat at the desk in the home office that, up until today, had served as their bedroom.

"I made a menu for a restaurant in town." She was just putting the finishing touches on her menu design for the Hilo café, shifting her drawings around the page until each one was in just the right place. "And look at this. I made coloring pages too."

Rory gasped theatrically and put her little hands over her heart. "For me?"

"Yep." She reached over to the printer and picked up the stack of drawings. There hadn't been room for all of her ideas on the menu, but they made fun coloring pages for kids. "Here you go."

"Thanks, Mama!" She grabbed the stack eagerly and lifted the pages up one by one, looking through the plants and animals that Lani had drawn.

"You're welcome, baby."

"Eep!" Rory squeezed her eyes closed when she got to the mako shark. "It's too scary!"

Lani laughed. "Sorry. Here. You want to color the hibiscus flowers?"

"No, I want to color the octopus."

"Great. Take them all out to your cousins, okay?"

"Okay!" She ran off, shouting for Lulu and Kiana.

Lani emailed the files to Tenn and then logged out of her accounts.

"You all packed up?" Mahina asked from the doorway.

"Hi Auntie. Yeah, we're all packed."

"We're gonna miss you."

Lani stood and hugged her aunt. "We're not going far."

"Still, it was nice to have you here."

"Thanks for giving us a place to land."

"Leilani!" 'Ōlena called from out front. "Emma's here."

She rolled her suitcases out through the front room, where Rory was coloring with her cousins. "Time to go, baby."

She gave her a stricken look. "But I'm not done with my octopus yet!"

"You can finish coloring at Auntie Emma's house. Come on."

"What's the rush?" Mahina asked. She turned to Emma as she walked in and asked, "Can you stay a while?"

"I would love to," Emma said. "Thank you. But we've got a new puppy in the car."

"Let him run around a while."

"I would, but I don't trust him around your chickens. And he's terrified of men."

"Not all sunshine and roses with the stray?" 'Ōlena asked.

Emma made a sound of frustration. "When we first got him to the house, he ran under Kai's bed and huddled in the corner.

Wouldn't even come out to pee. Then he finally came out to explore the yard this morning, and next thing I know he's in the street. I keep patching up the fence with scrap metal and he keeps finding new ways to get out. Lani, is this your car seat?"

"No, it's mine!" Rory giggled.

Lani picked up the car seat and walked out the front door. "I'll get it strapped in."

"I can get your luggage. Is this it?" Emma asked.

"Yep. All my worldly possessions." She opened the car door, and the dog shrank as far away from her as possible. She frowned and looked at Emma. "You're sure he's okay back here with the kids?"

"He's just shy," Kai said.

"He loves kids," Emma told her. "A neighbor came by with her two year old this morning. The kid was using him as a body pillow and he just lay there thumping his tail. The girls next door adore him, and he's so good with them. Then a man walks past the front fence and suddenly he's Cujo."

"That's not necessarily a bad thing," Lani told her.

"Yeah, tell that to the guy who lives across the street." She shrugged. "He's a work in progress."

"I want to see the puppy!" Rory climbed up into the seat and closed the door behind her. Through the window, Lani watched the dog unglue himself from the opposite side of the car and wriggle over to lick her outstretched hand.

They said their goodbyes – something that went on much longer than necessary, given that they were moving about five miles away – and got on the road.

"Does he have a name yet?" Lani asked.

"Mom called him Cujo," Kai said.

Emma snorted. "I was kidding. We're not naming our dog

Cujo."

"*You* said it. It's a good name!"

"Veto."

"Fine." Kai was quiet the rest of the drive. As soon as Emma stopped the car and Lani went to open the gate, Kai ran past her with the dog at his heels. He picked up a hammer and started banging it on a big lava rock.

"His new hobby," Emma said to Lani as she closed the gate.

"There are worse ways to work through his feelings." She watched him hit the rock over and over again, breaking off gravel-sized pieces. He had a pair of oversized sunglasses on as safety goggles. "At least he's taking them out on something inanimate."

"Come on, I'll help you carry your stuff up to your room."

The room that she would share with Rory was the only one on the third floor, a little tower at the back of the house. The windows had a spectacular view over the overgrown orchard all the way to the ohia trees at the back of the property. The fruit trees had been little more than saplings when she and Adam used to play back there. Now they were big enough to climb.

She was still unpacking when a shrieking ruckus started downstairs. She ran outside to see Kai chasing the puppy around the yard. The dog looked happy as could be, sure that they were playing some kind of game.

He had a fat gray chicken in his mouth.

"No!" Kai shouted. "No! Bad dog!"

"Cujo!" Emma rounded a corner of the house and popped out in front of the pup, who was startled into dropping the hen. "No!"

He ran off with his tail between his legs.

"Myrtle!" Kai cried, dropping to his knees next to the

chicken. He looked up at his mother, eyes filled with tears. "Is she dead?"

"I think she's just in shock." Emma picked the bird up gently. Myrtle roused herself and flapped her wings in a panic, but Kai was able to pin them to her sides and calm her. Rory crept closer, hands pressed to her face in fascinated horror.

"Is she injured?" Lani asked.

"I'm not sure." Emma gently shifted a wing to show a patch of bare skin. "When I found him, he had her pinned and he was pulling out mouthfuls of feathers with his teeth."

"Why is he so mean?" Kai asked tearfully.

"Oh, honey, he wasn't trying to be mean. He's just a puppy." She parted a patch of damp feathers on the other side to reveal a small flesh wound. "Would you run next door and ask to borrow that blue spray they used on the rooster?"

He ran off, and Emma looked at Lani.

"Farm life," she said with a sigh. "It's never boring."

Kai was back a minute later with a lanky girl of about eight. Her red hair was cut close to her head. Judging from the varying lengths and blunt lines, she had cropped it herself.

"I brought the blue spray," she announced.

"Thank you..." Emma paused, and the girl made a sour face.

"Piper." She pointed violently to her sheared hair for emphasis.

"Thank you, Piper." She accepted the little spray bottle and applied the antiseptic to the open wound, then covered the bald spot for good measure.

"Will that make her better?" Kai asked.

"It will help her heal, yes. She'll be okay."

"It also keeps the other chickens from eating her," Piper said matter-of-factly. Kai gave her a horrified look, and she shrugged. "It does."

Emma pressed her lips together. "She'll be fine, Kai."

"Do you want to help me find her some worms?" he asked Piper.

She blew out a noisy breath. "I wish. My dad says I have to do multiplication tables." She looked at Emma and held out a hand for the spray bottle. "We need that one. You can buy some at the farm store."

"I'll do that." She handed the bottle back, and Piper ran home.

"Can I help find worms?" Rory asked.

Kai shrugged, his expression grave. "Sure."

"I'm going to run to the store and pick up some of that spray," Emma said. "It's past time for me to get a collar and leash for that dog, too. And we're getting low on feed. Okay if I leave Kai here with you? Ten to one he'll still be digging in the mud when I get back."

Lani grinned. "Yeah, that's fine."

She finished unpacking and then went back out to check on the kids who, sure enough, were still digging in the mud. Kai had gathered an assortment of gardening tools, and they had about a dozen hens on standby waiting for worms.

As she watched, the puppy slunk towards them. Kai jumped up and brandished a trowel with a shout, and the dog shot off into the bushes.

"Kai!" she exclaimed. He dropped the trowel in surprise and turned to her with a guilty expression. "You scared him."

"Good," he said fiercely. Masking the guilt with anger.

"That's no way to teach a dog."

The scowl slipped, and his eyes filled with tears. "He tried to kill Myrtle."

Lani sighed and sat down on the muddy grass next to Rory. She patted the ground next to her and, after a moment's hesitation, Kai joined them.

"I've never had a dog before."

"I know, buddy. That was pretty scary, yeah? When he caught your chicken?"

Kai sniffed. "She's my favorite one."

"The thing is, that dog is just a baby. He's brand new, and he's still learning. He doesn't trust most people, but he had just started to trust you. Now, I don't know. Maybe he's not so sure."

He looked stricken. "What should I do?"

"You did a really amazing job yesterday. Why don't we go get some food, and you can do that again?"

"And then what?"

"Then we use the leash that your mom went to buy, and we hang out with the chickens. If he tries to chase them, we tell him no. When he's calm with the chickens, we give him treats."

"That's it?"

"That's it. And you know what?"

"What?"

"This kind of dog is really, really smart. They love to have a job. People buy them just to keep their other animals safe. So as soon as he realizes that the chickens are part of the family, he'll be their guard dog. He'll keep the mongooses away."

"What's a mongoose?"

Lani bit back a smile. Kai looked so much like his dad that sometimes it gave her a dizzy sense of *déjà vu*. It was difficult to remember that he hadn't grown up here.

"They're cute little rats," Rory said. "Like squirrels."

"Kind of," Lani said. "They're an invasive mammal that eats

meat."

"A carnivore!" Kai shouted like it was the answer to a trivia question.

"That's right, they're carnivores that eat baby chickens."

"Oh no!" Rory pressed her hands to her cheeks in playfully exaggerated horror, but Kai's expression was serious.

"And our dog will protect the chickens from mongooses?" he asked.

"That's the idea. He'll learn quick, you'll see. But we have to be kind. And he still needs a name."

He looked thoughtfully at the half-grown dog that was watching them from the bushes. "How about Diogee?"

"Diogee?"

"Yeah. Because dog is D-O-G. We can call him Dio."

She patted his back. "That's a great name."

Rory squeezed herself between them, plopping down on her mama's lap and crossing her arms. "Why does he get to name the dog?"

"You can name the chickens," she suggested.

"That one's Myrtle," Kai said, pointing to the tousled gray hen that stood some distance from the others. "But you can name the rest of them."

"Okay!" Rory jumped to her feet, which made the hens scatter. But they were back a moment later, walking cautiously forward, hopeful for more worms. She pointed to another gray hen, darker and more monotone than Myrtle. "That one is Bluey. And that red one is Bingo. And that's Muffin..."

Kai stood and looked down at Lani. "I'm going to go get some food for Dio."

She smiled and gave him the thumbs up.

"Mama!" Rory stomped her foot. "Are you even listening?"

She looked back at her. "I'm listening!"

"That one's Muffin." She pointed, frowned, and then pointed to an identical chicken. "No, wait, that one's Muffin. And that one is Socks." She paused her litany of chicken names and collapsed into Lani's lap, muddy and content.

"Hey Mama?"

"Yeah?"

"I like it here."

"Me too, baby. I like it here too."

12

Emma

Shoveling manure under the tropical sun was not how Emma pictured spending this stage of her life.

As strange as it was to be mucking out a goat pen in the middle of the Pacific, the truly surprising thing was how satisfying the work was.

She had taken to wearing John's old coveralls, sturdy things that had once been navy blue but had faded almost to a light gray over the years. The sun beat down on the top of her head, warming the bandana that she used to keep sweat out of her eyes. The muck boots that she'd bought at the farm store were a lifesaver when the yard turned muddy.

The goat paddock was overdue for a good mucking out. One wheelbarrow at a time, she transferred the round droppings and fallen feed out to the ever-hungry banana trees. The tropical heat and humidity alchemized things so quickly that she didn't bother with dedicated compost piles. They simply dumped their kitchen waste in low spots or at the base of trees, and the scraps turned to soil almost overnight.

"Mom!" Kai waved his arms at her from the other side of the gate in an impatient little dance. "Hey Mom!"

"What's up, kiddo?"

"I can't find Dio!"

"Did you check the gate?"

"Which gate?"

"The front gate!"

"Oh. No. I'll go check!" He raced off, gravel spraying out from under his shoes as he rounded the side of the house.

Emma took a breath and set her shovel aside. Where had Dio gotten through now?

She had used every bit of scrap metal laying around the property to patch up slumped and broken bits of fencing. The whole boundary line was a strange quilt of corrugated tin and heavy vines. And he still kept finding new ways to escape.

Their new puppy had escaped about a dozen times in the past few days, and every time he either came right back into the yard a minute later or circled around to the front gate and sat waiting to be let in. He seemed to enjoy identifying weaknesses in their perimeter, but he had no desire to leave this newfound haven of regular meals and cozy places to sleep.

She looked at the fence line for a minute, wondering what she had missed. Maybe she would walk the whole property boundary later. Or give Kai the job of tailing the dog and watching to see where he could still get out.

For now, she had a wheelbarrow full of high-quality fertilizer to feed the ten-foot papayas that were scattered here and there around the property. She pushed the wheelbarrow out of the goat paddock and closed the gate behind her.

Kai raced by with Diogee, who carried a fallen branch nearly as long as he was. They ran in circles around the huge catchment tank that provided all of their water.

Rain ran off the rooftop and into the catchment tank, where it was stored under cover to be pumped through a filter to the house. It was a comfort knowing that whatever happened, they had fresh water.

There were any number of things she loved about this life that she had never given much thought to before.

Feeling light with the sense of a task completed and heavy labor now done, she went inside to shed her filthy coveralls and take a hot shower.

Lani was busy in the kitchen, with four pots simmering away on the stove and counters full of prep work. The Madeira family was coming over today for a sort of house warming, Mahina and Manō and all the cousins, and Lani had been preparing food since dawn. Rory was set up at the kitchen table, coloring a new set of sea animals that Lani had drawn and printed.

They were still there when Emma came back down, showered and clean and ready to help.

"What are you making?"

"Chicken katsu and rice, and the 'ulu mac salad that my mom used to make." She paused to push a stray strand of hair back into her ponytail. "I haven't made this stuff in forever. It feels weird to make it alone. Bittersweet. Like it makes me feel closer to my mom, but at the same time it makes me miss her more."

She nodded sympathetically. "How can I help?"

"Do you want to shave this sweet onion?" Lani handed her a peeled Maui onion and a cheese grater, then showed her to a huge bowl full of cooked macaroni and bits of steamed breadfruit. "That's how my mom always did it."

"Of course." She tried shaving the onion directly over the bowl, then gave up and grabbed a cutting board so that she could brace the cheese grater on something.

"Mom, I'm bored!" Rory declared. She drew the words out, sounding so much like Kai that Emma winced. No one wanted their own kid to be the source of bad habits.

"Go outside," Lani told her.

"I don't like outside," she whined.

"You love outside. Go find some eggs."

"I don't like eggs." Rory hopped down from the chair and went to see what Lani was doing, but her mom swooped down to intercept her before she made it to the stove.

"Honey, I'm about to fry the chicken."

"I want to help!"

"No. I don't want you to get burned."

"I'm a good helper!"

"You are a very good helper, but the oil splashes when it gets hot, and the splashes burn. I don't want you to get a burn."

"I don't want to get a burn," Rory agreed, peering over her mom's shoulder at the pots on the stove. "I can make the salad?"

"Sure." Lani set Rory up at the kitchen table with a vegetable peeler and a pile of carrots, which the tiny girl proceeded to process with surprising dexterity.

"That's really good," Emma said.

"I'm good at peeling," Rory told her in a matter-of-fact tone.

"I should invite Kai into the kitchen more." She scraped the shredded onions into the bowl of macaroni and stirred it all together.

"She was always with me," Lani said, eyes on the chicken that she was frying on the stove. "She wanted to help in the kitchen. Eventually I realized how capable she is. She's good with a knife, even. I just wouldn't give her one while I'm busy frying food."

"What's next for the mac salad?"

"An absurd amount of mayonnaise."

"Ha, okay. On it."

'Ōlena's minivan pulled up just as Lani was finishing the last of the chicken. Lulu and Kiana spilled through in a wave of energy, sweeping Rory up in the general excitement. 'Ōlena and her parents came through a moment later, and the front room filled with warm greetings.

"Is Kekoa still coming?" Lani asked.

"He should be here any minute," 'Ōlena said. "He wouldn't skip out on free food."

"Don't talk about your brother like that," Mahina scolded. "He's a business owner and a single father, not some lazy teenager."

"Where's the lie, though?"

Mahina gave her daughter a playful shove and walked through to the kitchen.

"This all looks amazing!" she said.

"Just some basics," Lani said.

"Did you put *'ulu* in this mac salad? This is your grandma's recipe, isn't it?"

"Is it?" Lani grinned. "I tried to make it like my mom used to."

"Yep, and she made it just like our mom did." Mahina patted Lani's cheek. "She would be so proud of you. They both would, your mom and your grandma."

She blinked rapidly, smiling through her tears. "Thanks, Auntie."

Mahina turned to Emma. "Before I forget, come out to the

car. I have something for you."

They walked out through the front door, and Emma blinked in the sudden sunlight. Mahina opened up the back of ʻŌlena's minivan to reveal a huge cardboard box full of roots and twigs and bits of vine.

"I, um, thank you?" Emma couldn't keep a bit of uncertainty from creeping into her tone, and Mahina chuckled.

"It's all plants that grow from cuttings. There's plenty of green in John's garden, but it's all weeds. I thought you'd want to start fresh. These slips are *uala*, sweet potatoes. There's white, orange, and you know da purple kine? That's this one.

"These seeds are ice cream bean, they grow quick as anything. What else? There's taro corms. This one here is cassava. This is chaya. Here's some bele. What else, what else...?"

She picked up a bundle of green twigs about as wide as their pinky fingers. Mahina had trimmed off most of the leaves, leaving just a few at the end of each branch. She plucked one of these off and handed it to Emma.

"This is katuk, it's a tasty perennial. Taste it."

Obediently, Emma put the nondescript green leaf in her mouth and chewed. It was surprisingly tender. The taste was pleasant, almost nutty.

"It's good cooked. I like to put it in soup." Mahina held up another bundle of twigs and smiled. "And these are hibiscus. Every color I have. A woman needs some flowers."

"And I just... stick them in the dirt?"

"Yep. Just plant them and keep the weeds away. It helps to mulch them real good. And make sure you plant them deep enough, maybe halfway in the ground."

"Thank you so much." She hefted the heavy box, overwhelmed by the bounty.

"Just put it somewhere shady until you're ready to plant. And if they don't take the first time, don't worry. Just tell me and I'll bring more. They don't cost nothing."

"And you said that there's a garden?" Emma asked hesitantly. "I'm not sure where you mean."

Mahina barked with laughter. "It's that far gone, huh? Here, you tuck that box in the car port and I'll show you where the garden is."

They walked around to the back of the house, to a lush green area that Emma hadn't looked twice at. Mahina pushed aside some of the weeds to reveal a garden gate, and they walked around the perimeter. It was the size of her backyard in Redwood Grove, and the whole area was fenced; the fence was just so completely overgrown and green that Emma hadn't seen it.

"This isn't a weed," Mahina warned, parting a section of broad green leaves to reveal a spectacular purple passionfruit flower. "Don't pull the *liliko'i* vines."

"Wouldn't dream of it," Emma agreed. Standing close and looking closer, she could see the regular lines of mounded green where the earth rose in garden beds.

"The weeds took over, but it's worth clearing them out. There's good soil underneath. Dirt's a big deal here, you know. This neighborhood is all rock. Basically they just built houses on a lava field. John had this soil delivered by the truckload for his garden beds."

She was quiet then, probably thinking about her late brother.

"I'm sorry that we didn't come to visit more," Emma said quietly. "We always meant to, but there was always something... Work, money, Kai. It's crazy how fast the years pile up."

"I get it. We talked all the time about going to see Lani in Alaska, but we never made it happen. I still feel terrible about that, leaving her all alone up there." Mahina put an arm around her. "You've got nothing to feel bad about. It's not like John put a whole lot of effort into going to see his grandson. You're a mama, you were busy taking care of your own little family. Those early days take everything you've got. I remember, believe me. It's the grandparents' job to put the effort in. Of course, that's easy for me to say, with my grandbabies all right there with me. Manō and I are lucky."

"Kai is hurting so much," she confided. Tears ran down her face as months of grief welled up and spilled over. "I don't know how to help him."

"You're doing exactly right. You're here. He has people all around him, people who knew his dad. Most important, he has you. You're with him every day, loving him through it. It just takes time. Healing is a slow, unsteady thing."

"Yeah." Emma sniffed and wiped the tears from her face. "Thanks again for the cuttings. I'm just starting to get the hang of daily farm chores, and it's all done me a lot of good. Clearing out this garden sounds like the perfect project."

"Good." Mahina squeezed her arm and released her. "Come on inside. I'm gonna eat a whole plate of that mac salad."

13

Lani

Lani drove slowly across the high, flat plains of Hawai'i. It was a perfect day, vivid blue skies with fluffy white clouds. They'd left the dreary gray skies of the east side behind for a Kona beach day.

The Saddle Road had taken them through a stark landscape of black lava rock and scrappy red plants, and now they were coasting through the green hills and plains that sat just above Kona.

Cars swerved around her, racing across the island at top speed, but she was in no hurry. The scenery was beautiful, and they'd found a working radio station that played local country music. The kids were content to eat their snacks and stare out the windows after a pit stop at the Mauna Kea Recreation Area, which had a great playground smack in the middle of nowhere, with biting winds and a gorgeous view of the *mauna*.

There were any number of beaches to choose from on the Kona side, but most of them were either crowded or required a serious hike across vast fields of lava rock to access.

Lani and Emma opted for one of the northern beaches that was easy to get to but not too terribly crowded, with relatively calm water and plenty of shade.

The generous trees that rooted and grew in the sandy beaches were as astonishing to Lani as the trees that grew on solid rock. She didn't know how they managed it, but she was grateful for the shelter they provided from the hot Kona sunshine. Even a blue-sky day in Hilo had nothing on Kona sunlight, magnified as it was by the pale sands and turquoise waters.

Black sand beaches could get scorching hot, but at least they didn't burn you indirectly the way white sand beaches could. Not that Lani burned too easily, but she wasn't so sure about her Alaska-born baby or auburn-haired Emma. Even she could pick up a sunburn in Kona if she wasn't careful, especially after so many years away.

The past few weeks under the cool gray skies and intermittent winter sunlight of the east side hadn't done much to restore her tan. Her healthy island coloring was coming back, but slowly.

"This is taking forever," Rory whined from the back seat.

"It's a long drive, huh?" Lani agreed. "We're almost there."

They were just starting to coast down the steep slope that led down to Waikoloa, so 'almost there' was an overstatement, at least to a four year old. She felt along the side pocket in the driver-side door of the truck, looking for Rory's favorite CD.

"This music is terrible," Kai said as the country station started to crackle. "Can we listen to something fun?"

"You read my mind, cuz." She found her old *Moana* CD and popped that in.

Rory spent the rest of the drive belting off-key showtunes, which made time go quicker... for her, at least.

Finally they pulled into the long parking lot at the family-friendly beach they had chosen. There were tons of other young families there already, unloading the piles of chairs and floaties that they found necessary for a day at the beach. Lani and Emma had erred on the side of simplicity, with just an old sheet to sit on a small cooler full of food and drinks.

They were stuck for a minute while Emma wrestled sunscreen onto Kai, and Lani took the chance to look at her phone. It had been buzzing intermittently throughout their drive, but she'd ignored it.

She checked her messages now. There were a few from 'Ōlena, replying to Lani's message asking if she had any Costco requests. They would take the opportunity of being on this side of the island to stock up on some inexpensive staples.

There were *also* – and she deliberately ignored these until she had replied to her cousin – texts from Tenn.

Just got a big batch of menus printed! Couldn't be more perfect!

He'd included a picture of the menu she had designed, printed on quality cardstock. Then a picture of her coloring pages, filled with careful color or wild scribbles and taped in positions of honor along the walls of his restaurant.

When are you coming to see them in person?

Lunch tomorrow, maybe, she replied. *We're Kona side today.*

See you tomorrow, then. His reply came through immediately. *Enjoy the sunshine! It's pouring over here.*

"What are you grinning about?" Emma teased her.

She put her phone away. "Nothing."

"Hmm." Emma made a knowing sound, still smiling.

"Can we *go* now?" Rory demanded.

"Yep." She tossed her sunscreen back in her beach bag. "Let's go swimming!"

"Yay!" Rory jumped down from the truck.

"Yay," Kai said in a tone that was pure Eeyore.

The water shone with blinding light, and they walked down the beach to find a spot that would stay shady all day. Kai hovered near the trunk of the large tree, peering cautiously out at the other beachgoers in the surf. Rory, on the other hand, plunged immediately into the water.

Lani stood just behind her daughter, in the surf up to her knees, while Rory let the waves push her forward and backward. She cackled with delight when a particularly rough one tumbled her, and then she ran right back into the surf.

Eventually Emma coaxed Kai out past the breaking waves and into calmer water, where she stood steady and held him up. He would swim a bit, floating over the easy waves that passed without breaking, and then reach out to his mom.

Rory wanted to go out into the deep water too, and so Lani helped her out past the shorebreak. Her tiny daughter refused to be carried, so Lani just stayed next to her and held her steady as she ducked under the rolling whitewater of each oncoming wave.

The swim out to her cousin was so exhausting that she finally did let her mother hold her when they were past the shorebreak.

Then, once she had caught her breath, she swam circles around them.

When they finally went in to shore and settled onto their picnic blanket in the shade, the kids ate with the ferocious appetite unique to growing children who had spent hours in the water.

Once their bellies were full, they went to the wet sand just beyond the surf and set to designing their own civilization in miniature.

Rory constructed a whole village of fairy houses, complete with doors and chimneys made from bits of seaweed and fallen twigs. She used small stones to create paths leading from one door to the next and adorned each little sandhouse with shells.

While she made the village, Kai dedicated his efforts to a wall and a moat that would protect the villagers against the incoming tide. He worked tirelessly, digging deep into the sand and building a wall that extended far beyond the village on either side. It even curved towards the sea on either end, the better to divert water away from the fairy houses.

Lani felt a peculiar ache in her chest, watching them.

She felt as though she had fallen through a time warp to some long-ago day when her parents were still alive, when they used to swing by and pick Adam up on their way out of Hilo, escaping the rainy winter weather in favor of a beach day on the west side of the island.

Rory and Kai looked so much like her and Adam that it gave her a peculiar sense of *déjà vu*, like watching her childhood from the outside.

During those lonely years in Alaska, she'd felt a growing sense of guilt for not giving Rory a sibling. Lani herself was happy with her perfect little girl, content to give her everything that she had. But at the same time, she felt like she was cheating her daughter out of some vital piece of her childhood, a relationship that would last forever.

By the time that she was married and physically ready to have a second baby, she had begun to have her doubts about Zeke. And by the time he had quit his shipboard job to live fulltime in Alaska, she had known deep down that she couldn't tie herself to him with a baby that was his by blood. He had pestered her for a baby, but she stood firm.

Even when that pestering had turned into something scarier. Especially then.

It was bad enough that Rory had spent her early years under the same roof as that volatile temper; Lani wouldn't knowingly bring another baby into that.

All the same, she had felt a deep grief – wishing that things were different, that she had more to offer her daughter than the life of an only child. She knew that feeling all too well.

Her own mother had suffered one miscarriage after another, something that she became aware of very gradually as a little girl. At times she felt surrounded by the spirits of her brothers and sisters.

It had been a comfort to her, in a strange way, the felt experience of a young child who couldn't understand the full picture, could only grasp the vague imprint of siblings who never quite materialized. Sometimes she worried that she was condemning her daughter to the same, long days with only ghosts for company.

But ever since moving home to Hawai'i, her guilt had receded. She watched 'Ōlena's daughters dote on Rory, watched Kai slowly come out of his shell, saw the growing community of the co-op her cousin had created, and she knew that Rory wasn't doomed to a lonely childhood.

It wasn't the same as having a sister, sharing a room and a life the way Lulu and Kiana did, but that way okay. Maybe it was even better, judging by the way 'Ōlena's daughters scrapped like cats in a sack and then doted on their little cousin. That was the relationship that Lani had with her cousins growing up: all the love of siblings without the scrappy complications that came from living in close quarters year after year.

Hours later, when the kids had burned off nearly all of their energy, Lani and Emma loaded them back into the car and headed south for their big grocery run.

They finished with just enough time left to catch the day's sunset. The kids were already nodding off in the back seat, but Emma insisted that they drive down to the beach.

"I love it here," she said, "but I've missed ocean sunsets so much. I've never lived on the east coast of anywhere before, it's so strange."

Not one to turn down a sunset, particularly a Kona sunset, Lani was content to drive a few miles down Queen Ka'ahumanu Highway and turn into the harbor.

They parked at the far end and walked a short distance along the coast, each carrying their overtired kiddos, until they reached a hidden beach that ran for nearly a mile up the coast.

The kids perked up again as soon as they reached the beach, and they splashed happily in the shallows while Lani and Emma settled down to watch the sunset.

The sky turned yellow and gold as their piece of the globe turned slowly away from the sun, and the colors only intensified after the sun disappeared. The whole sky turned gold with vivid pink clouds that faded to lavender if they looked back towards home.

Rory came back shivering, and Lani wrapped her in a thick towel. It was funny how quickly her Alaska baby had turned into an island girl. Though she supposed she always had her in soft merino thermals up north. Even this far south, the water felt cold in the wintertime.

Kai wasn't shivering, but his lips tinged towards blue as the light faded from the sky. His mother bundled him up as well, drying his hair and then pulling a hooded beach towel over his head.

"Can we come back tomorrow?" he asked as they walked back towards the parking lot.

"I don't know about tomorrow," Emma said with a light laugh, "but we can definitely drive over here more often. There are so many amazing places on this island that we haven't been to yet!"

"I just want to come here," Kai said, suddenly stubborn. Emma sighed and exchanged a look with Lani, mustering her patience before replying.

"We can definitely come here again soon."

"Thanks." Kai slipped his hand into Emma's, a simple gesture that touched Lani's heart. Rory was quick to grab Kai's other hand, and then she reached out for her mom.

They finished out their day like that, the four of them walking hand in hand under a pink and purple sky.

14

Emma

Another crack of thunder shook the house, and Emma peeked into her son's room. Incredibly, he was still asleep. The poor dog had retreated to the far corner beneath Kai's bed, and he showed no inclination of emerging before the storm passed. Outside, the pouring rain merged with the waterfall sound of the catchment tank overflowing.

The wind screamed past the windows, but it was a bit quieter in here. His room was under Lani's, so the rain wasn't landing directly overhead. The noise in *her* bedroom was like standing under a waterfall with a bucket over her head.

Drowning in white noise, she paced through the dark house like a ghost.

It had been a good day. Full and busy, fulfilling. She'd fallen asleep easily not long after Kai.

Then she dreamt of Adam. A golden, shining nothing of a dream. She could only remember the radiant happiness of being with him, seeing his face, leaning into the sturdy solidity of his body.

Then she woke up.

And she missed him with an excruciating intensity that she hadn't experienced in weeks. There was no sleeping after that.

The lights blazed on, and she flinched.

"Emma?" Lani stood at the lightswitch, watching her with a worried expression. "Are you okay?"

"I'm fine," she said automatically.

Her chin dropped a bit, and she gave her an earnest look. "Really?"

"No, not really."

She nodded and crossed to the kitchen counter. "Do you want some tea?"

"Sure. Thank you."

"We have to figure out what all is growing here. Because I don't know much about herbs, and I still found a bunch of plants growing. There must be others I didn't recognize. I picked this *māmaki* and lemongrass earlier." She put huge green leaves and chopped rounds of grass into a pot. "There's hibiscus back there too, the kind you use for tea."

"I'd love to learn more about the plants that are growing here."

Lani's voice and the everyday kitchen clatter cut through the haze of her grief, pushing the pain back until her thoughts were coherent again.

The ache for her husband was still there, like a phantom limb that pained her constantly. But engaging with the world, this place, kept it under control.

With the kitchen lights on, she could see puddles on the kitchen floor. She looked up and saw a drop of water fall from a damp spot on the ceiling.

"We've got a leak."

"Yeah, there's one in my room too. I put a pitcher under it."

Emma looked out the window and watched the rain flying sideways. "How do the chickens get through these hurricanes?"

Lani burst out laughing.

"What?"

"You think this is a hurricane? This is *not* a hurricane."

Another crack of thunder shook the house. "Close enough."

Lani shook her head, but she didn't argue. The pot on the stove started to simmer, and she turned it off. Lemongrass-scented steam filled the air.

Emma mopped up the puddle and set a pot on top. The steady ding of water drops was swallowed by the raging storm outside. When she looked back at Lani, she was looking down at her phone with a stricken expression.

"What's wrong?"

Lani shook her head quickly, like she was shaking herself out of a daze. "My ex." She turned her phone off and put it in the far corner of the kitchen.

"What about him?" Emma asked.

"More threats." She pulled two mugs down from the cupboard and filled each of them with tea. "I blocked him on everything. I got a new phone number. Then he made new accounts so that he could spam me on socials. I should just get off of all of them altogether."

"This is Rory's father?"

"Not exactly." They carried their tea into the living room, where the noise of the storm wasn't quite as loud. Lani blew on her tea, looking off into middle distance.

"We worked on ships together," she began. "Me and Zeke. Cruise ship culture was very work hard, party hard. It was fun for a while. I was just getting out of college, trying to escape myself. I think that's why I stayed away for as many years as I did. With my parents both gone and Adam in California, no place felt like home anymore.

"Anyway, we drank a lot. We were only allowed beer and wine on the ship – though of course plenty of people snuck booze on too - but in port we really cut loose.

"Rory's father was an Italian guy I met in Greece. A one night stand. I don't even know his last name. By the time I realized I was pregnant, we were long gone. I had no way of finding him again.

"Rory's 'Dad'," she continued with heavy air quotes, "was a coworker of mine. He heard me crying to a friend about it, because I didn't know what to do. I had only ever worked on ships, and I'd gone up pretty far. Managing my department on the boat, you know? No chance of doing that with a baby.

"I could have come home to Hawai'i, but... I don't know. Showing up pregnant, no idea of who the father was, it was a humiliating prospect. And I wasn't ready to give up the career I had dedicated my whole adult life to. I'd never planned on having kids."

Lani paused and sipped her tea before she continued. Outside, the wind picked up to a frenzied whine as it grazed the side of the house.

"Zeke owned property in Alaska, an old family place. He said I could stay there a while, rent free. I spent a few summers working on ships up in Alaska, and a big group of us spent a week up at his cabin once. It's so beautiful up there. A friend said she would help me, take time off between contracts and be there when the baby was born.

"I was—" Lani's voice cracked and she looked down, pulling

at a loose thread on her pajamas. "The idea was to have the baby there and give her up for adoption. So I could go back to work."

She squeezed her eyes shut and took a long, shuddering breath.

"We had the nicest family lined up, this older couple who lived a little ways south of there. I had my doubts the whole time, but I tried to ignore them, to talk myself out of them. I had this whole plan, you know? I was a couple years away from being an operations manager. A decade of that and I could have retired so young. I had it all planned out.

"And then I met Rory." Tears spilled from her eyes, and she smiled. Emma reached out and took her hand. "She was born at night, at home. The northern lights were going crazy outside, and I stood in front of these huge windows watching them. Then I held her for the first time, and I just... I knew I could never let her go."

She wiped the tears from her face and grabbed a tissue for her nose.

"And Zeke?" Emma asked.

"He said I could stay as long as I needed. I had plenty of savings for groceries and stuff, so I wasn't worried about finding work right away. I just spent those first months in this happy little cocoon with my baby. I was so in love with her."

She sighed, and her expression darkened. "Then Zeke proposed. And I said yes. I'm not sure why, exactly. I wasn't in love with him. I mean, I was fond of the guy. We had worked together on and off for years. And I was grateful. But I think... deep down, I think I was scared that he was the best I could do. For me, for Rory... Here I was with this baby, and there was this man on one knee offering to be her father, and... I said yes.

"It was okay, for a while. Zeke was at work three months out of four, and I was home with Rory all the time. I loved it. And he was nice enough, when he was home. It felt cozy. Domestic.

"Then he stopped working. More and more, he had been obsessing over what I did when he was gone. He was scared I was seeing someone, which was crazy. I was with Rory literally all the time. She would only sleep on top of me. But he quit his shipboard job and came home full time.

"Things got steadily worse after that."

"Worse how?" Emma asked.

Lani shrugged and looked away. She was quiet for a while, the sound of the storm outside taking over.

Eventually she said, "I stayed longer than I should have. It got bad enough that Rory was terrified. I couldn't hide it from her anymore. He would go ballistic at bedtime, screaming at us and slamming doors because Rory wanted me to sleep with her, and he wanted me in bed with him. He would always apologize the next morning. Sometimes he'd cry and beg me to stay.

"Then one night, he dragged me out by my hair. He slammed the door and locked Rory in the dark. She was screaming for me, terrified, but he wouldn't let me go to her."

A single tear fell, and Emma squeezed her hand."

"We left the next day," Lani continued, "while he was out at a construction job he'd picked up. We stayed a few nights with some old friends in Juneau. I hadn't seen them in ages, hadn't seen anyone. Zeke didn't like it. But they let us stay with them, even drove me down to the courthouse so I could file for divorce. And then they drove us to the airport."

"I'm glad that you're here." Emma put an arm around her

and they sank deeper into the old sofa.

"Ditto."

There was another crash of thunder, so close that it came in the same moment as the lightning and shook the walls. The lights cut out, plunging them into complete darkness.

"Shoot," Lani said. "Do you have your phone on you?"

"No, but I have a flashlight on my keychain. It's hanging near the door."

She stood and walked with exaggerated caution towards the front door, still not familiar enough with this house to find her way in the dark.

Another flash of lightning lit up the house for a second, long enough for her to orient herself. She made it to the door and fumbled along the wall until her fingers found the familiar shape of her keychain.

The little flashlight put out a narrow beam of light that enabled her to find the candles and matches she'd come across earlier that week while she was cleaning the kitchen. Once the first was lit, Lani used the tiny flashlight to check on both of the kids while Emma lit more candles downstairs.

"Both still sound asleep," she said as she came back down.

"Once Kai is asleep, he's out. He'll sleep through fireworks, anything. I still have to wake him up at two in the morning to pee, or he'll sleep through that too."

"Rory's the same way. She'll sleep through anything. I can't remember the last time I slept like that." She was quiet while she poured two fresh mugs of tea. Then she said, "I have nightmares."

"Me too."

"He knows I'm from Hawai'i. I keep waiting for him to show up. He doesn't have our address, but I keep expecting to run into him in town. I'll see someone who's the same height as him or has the same hair, just a glimpse, and my brain clicks into panic mode."

"I'm so sorry," Emma told her. "I'm sorry that we didn't stay in touch. We were all wrapped up in our own life, to the point that it became a joke in my family. We lived in the same little town as them and I was still the absent sister, off in my own little world. It was always just me and Adam, and then me and Adam and Kai."

"It's not your fault."

"But we should have tried harder. We should have known what was happening and been there for you."

"I didn't want anyone to know. I felt so ashamed. And it happened so gradually that half the time I questioned my own sanity. He *made* me question my own sanity. Gaslighting, love bombing. Emotional abuse.

"I kept in touch with some of my friends, and eventually I opened up to a couple of them, enough for them to have some idea of what was going on. They sent me memes, videos, articles. It gave me names for what was happening to me, made me feel less alone.

"I could have reached out to family. I could have come home to Hawai'i a long time ago. Or even California; I knew that you and Adam would have taken us in if I'd asked. But I hated that orphan feeling. I didn't want to be the family charity case.

"I don't know why I thought that living with Zeke was any better. Maybe because he wanted me there so badly. It didn't feel like pity or charity, not at first.

"Later, of course, he was happy to lord it over me, everything that he had done for us. But in the beginning, he made it seem like *I* was doing *him* the favor by staying there. And I was convinced for a while that we could make a go of it. Be the happy little family, give my daughter the father that I robbed her of by being so irresponsible."

"Don't do that to yourself," Emma said.

"But it's true. I was reckless. I haven't had another drink since, not since Rory."

Emma reached out and took her hand. "You're an amazing mom. She adores you. And you're so good with her, with all of the kids."

"That's what I did on the cruise ships."

"You worked with kids?"

Lani nodded and wiped her eyes. When she spoke again, her voice was brighter. "I worked in the kids club. It was a great job, up at the top of the ship with gorgeous views when nearly everyone else was stuck below deck. Just playing with kids all day. Eventually I ran the kids club on one ship after another, all over the world."

"What about now? Do you want to go back to working with kids?"

She thought about that for a moment. "Not really. Being with Rory every day takes everything I've got and then some. I can't imagine working with kids and being a single mom. That sounds doubly exhausting. I don't know how 'Ōlena does it."

"I hear that. Before I had Kai, I had so much patience. I love kids." She chuckled ruefully and admitted, "I thought that being a mom would be easy. But the older he gets, the harder it is. I have to work hard to stay patient now, even with other kids. I'm just tapped out. And since Adam, well." She stared down into her tea as shame seeped through her chest. "I've lost my patience with Kai so many times."

"That's understandable."

"Not to him." She looked back up at Lani and changed direction. "So what do you want to do?"

"I don't know. I can't go back to working on cruise ships. It would kill me to go months without seeing Rory, even if I did have someone who was willing to take care of her for that amount of time. There are plenty of similar jobs on island, but not near here. I'm lucky to have a job at all, and serving up shave ice is kind of fun for now. But long term... I have no idea."

"You'll figure it out. You have time."

"What about you?"

"What about me?"

"You were a kindergarten teacher before Kai, right?"

"I was." She had taught a few different grades over the years, and she'd loved it. She loved the kids, their endless curiosity. But fighting for the best interests of her students in a system that seemed designed to crush their spirits had been exhausting. She had been happy to leave it behind for motherhood, determined to keep Kai out of the system that she had worked in.

"Will you ever go back to teaching?" Lani asked.

"I don't think so. Maybe someday."

"What's next for you?"

"I have no idea. I'm still in survival mode. I mean, I have everything that I need. I'm so lucky in that way. I can't imagine struggling to pay the bills at the same time as I'm navigating this kind of grief." She paused, thinking. "Or, I don't know, maybe that would have helped. Having work to do here, just the daily tasks that have to get done like milking the goats and all of that, it does seem to help. It gets me past that crippling inertia that pinned me down at home.

"I still wake up feeling that same crippling grief and anxiety, and I lay in bed thinking that I don't want to be here. Honestly, the only thing that kept me here once Adam was gone was knowing that I had to keep going for Kai. But now, it only takes me a minute to pull myself up out of that and step out into the sunlight and go milk those damn goats. I don't think that I could have gotten so far so quickly without that immediate driver of another being needing me. Which sounds terrible, because obviously Kai needed me. And of course I kept him fed and everything. But what he needed was more than I could give. And what this place asks of me is just right. It keeps me moving."

"So are you going to stay?"

The question surprised her, though it shouldn't have. Part of the medicine in this place was the opportunity to exist in the present, a string of moments, without worrying too much about the future. The idea had always been to come for a short stay and set things to rights. But now that she was here, she had zero desire to book that flight home.

"My family is still asking me every day when I'll be back. I can't stay forever. We have our house there, and I have a nephew arriving any day. But I think we'll stay for a while. I'm not in a hurry to find someone to rent or run the place, which was the original plan. Of course, it's yours if you want it."

Lani rocked backwards in surprise.

"Legally it's Kai's when he turns eighteen, but that's a long way off. We'll need a caretaker. You don't have to decide now, but if you do want to stay in the area, you're welcome to it."

"This place means a lot to me," Lani said, her voice hoarse. "I would love to stay here."

"We can fix up both of the houses," Emma told her, thinking out loud, "and maybe rent out one or the other. Vacation rental, maybe... or maybe not. Even renting to a local family should be more than enough to pay for property taxes and maintenance. But that's all a ways away."

"I'm not sure that I could manage it all on my own. Working and taking care of Rory, plus the goats and all? Keeping the jungle from taking over? It's a lot."

"It is." Emma smiled broadly, though she couldn't have said what it was about this mess that so delighted her.

She leaned back and sipped the delicious tea that Lani had made. It made her think of her big sister, both the homegrown tea and the comfortable silence. The *māmaki* tasted similar to the nettle that Toni used as a base in so many of her mixes. She loved her sister's blends, but this simple pairing fresh from their own backyard was something else entirely.

"Anyway," Lani said after a while, "I like having you here."

"Ditto." Emma took a deep breath of the warm, bright lemongrass steam. "Kai and I will be here for a while yet. For right now, this is where we need to be."

15

Lani

Hurricane it was not, but the storm did some damage. The ground was littered with broken branches, and there were huge damp spots on the ceiling. The roof was off of the hen house, but the chickens had gotten through just fine. They'd sheltered in the huge banyan tree near the back of the property, a monster of a thing so thick and wide that the ground around its twisting trunk was barely damp.

Puddles the size of ponds were quickly shrinking as the rainwater filtered through the thin soil and sank into the volcanic rock below.

In the meantime, the ducks were having the time of their life in one particularly deep bit of flooded yard, and the kids were shrieking with laughter as they ran through the puddles.

The day had barely started, and already the sun was breaking through the clouds. A vibrant rainbow arced over the farm and disappeared into the ohia forest beyond.

"Have you seen Dio?" Emma had gone full farmer in rain

boots and coveralls. "I think he got out again. I thought that I had found all of the holes in the fence line, but I must have missed at least one."

"He jumped!" Rory landed in a nearby puddle with a great splash, spraying them both.

"Who jumped?" Lani asked.

"Dio did!" She pointed to a section of fencing that had been brought low by a thick mat of weedy vines. "He jumped right there!"

Emma made a frustrated sound. "That's where the goats got over. I should have realized that he could jump it too."

"Rory," Lani said, "you have to tell me or Auntie if you see any of the animals get out like that."

She stomped her foot with a splash. "I did tell you!"

"You have to tell us right away."

She shrugged, unrepentant. "I forgot."

Emma trudged towards the front gate. "I'm about ready to drop him back where I found him."

"You don't mean that," Lani said, walking with her.

"No, I don't." She sighed. "I'm going to go see if I can find him."

"I'll come with you. He never goes far."

They rounded a stand of greenery that hid the house from the street and there he was, sitting on the other side of the gate, waiting patiently to be let in. His tail wagged excitedly as they approached, and his tongue lolled out of his mouth.

Emma laughed and opened the gate. He ran through and circled her twice before bolting off to join the kids in their play.

"Still want to dump him at Keiki Beach?" Lani teased.

"Never."

Lani's phone rang and she checked the screen. "Just a sec,

it's Manō."

"'Ōlena's dad?"

"Yeah." She picked up. "Hey Uncle, howzit?"

"Leilani! How you doin after that storm? John's roof still leaking everywhere?"

"It's leaking in a few places, yeah."

"I told him ten times we could fix it, but he always said he'd do it himself. I'll come today with Kekoa. We'll get that roof fixed before we get a real storm."

"Thanks, Uncle." She hung up and smiled at Emma. "He's going to come by later and deal with the leaks in the roof."

Emma's eyes widened. "He doesn't have to do that."

Lani was puzzled by her surprise. She had been a Kealoha long enough to know what *'ohana* meant.

"Family looks out for each other. Adam would have done the same for them."

"That's true."

Manō showed up that afternoon with half the family in tow. They climbed right up on the roof and patched the leaks, but they didn't stop there. Kekoa and his friends cut out collapsed pieces of fencing and replaced them.

'Ōlena came by at the end of the day. She found John's weed eater and used it to carve paths through the overgrowth. Her girls ran barefoot along the gravel paths, all smiles and excitement until Kiana fell backwards with a shocked cry.

"My foot!" She cradled her bare foot between her hands and looked at the sole.

"Kiana!" her mom called from across the yard. "How many times I gotta tell you to wear your slippahs?"

"What happened? Oh, *hilahila*!" Lulu dropped to her knees for a better look at the low-growing weed. It snaked across dirt and gravel, and the tiny thorns on its stems packed a punch. But kids loved its responsive, delicate leaves. "Kiki, look!"

She brushed one tiny branch and the plant responded immediately: each pair of leaflets folded together rapidly, one after another. Kiana copied her, poking at another cluster of leaflets and watching with a scowl as it folded in on itself.

"Auntie," she said severely, looking up at Lani. "You're supposed to kill *hilahila*."

"No!" her sister cried, putting her hands over the spiny weed protectively.

"Yes!" Kiana said fiercely.

"It's not the plant's fault you stepped on her!"

"Is too!"

"I'll pull up the ones in the path," Lani promised, "but I need some gloves."

"I won't let you kill her." Lulu stood between her auntie and the thorny weed. Lani gave her a long, level look... and then she let the subject drop. She could easily wait until another day to pull weeds.

A familiar truck pulled up out front, and suddenly Lani's entire focus was there beyond the fence.

Dio ran up to the gate, snapping and snarling the way he had the first time he saw Manō and Kekoa. Kai ran over and managed to calm him down, though he still growled low in his throat as Tenn walked around the back of his truck.

Olivia hopped out and was greeted with shrieks of excitement from the other girls. Even Kiana ran up and vied for her attention, injured foot forgotten. Lulu opened the front gate for her as Tenn pulled two paper bags out of the back of his truck.

Lani walked up to the gate. "What are you doing here?"

"Hello to you too."

She waited, hands on her hips.

"I came to give the guys a hand with the roof, but it looks like they were too quick for me." He looked over her shoulder to where Manō was climbing down from the roof. "I got stuck at work. I figured I could at least bring lunch. And these"

He reached into the cab of his truck and pulled out a stack of papers. They were high-quality card stock. On them, he had printed her new menus.

"Wow," she breathed, startled to see her work come to life. "They look great."

"They're perfect. And the coloring pages were a nice touch. Thank you."

"It was a fun project. I sketched too many things, more than I could reasonably fit on the menus. But I didn't want them to go to waste, and you know how much kids love coloring sheets. We'll even choose one restaurant over another based on that, because Rory gets so excited. Forget the twenty coloring books she has at home. It's all about those restaurant placemats."

"Yeah, Olivia too." He smiled, and his singular focus was like sun through a magnifying glass. Dazzling. Dangerous.

Lani was too busy putting out the last fire to let a new one start.

"So what do I owe you?" he asked.

She shook her head. "Nothing."

"I have to pay you for your work."

"Really, it was nothing. It's just some doodles."

"Don't do that to yourself."

"What?"

"This is your work. Your time, your talent. You are amazing at what you do. Don't diminish it like that."

Lani looked over to where the kids were swinging on vines. "I'm not going to take your money."

"Free meals for life then."

She looked back at him and tried not to smile. "That's ridiculous."

"Free lunch for a year?"

"Lunch for a month," she countered.

"You know that negotiations generally work the opposite way, right?"

She smiled and looked away.

"Tenn! Howzit?" Kekoa walked up and greeted him with a back-slapping hug.

"I brought some boar burgers for you and your dad."

"*Mahalo*, brah." He took both bags and walked off, shouting for his dad.

"There's, ah, food in there for you too." Tenn grinned at Lani, just making glancing eye contact before turning back to his truck. Was *he* nervous? He reached in through the window and pulled out a bottle of cane juice. "And this."

"Thank you." She accepted the drink, at a loss for what else to say.

"You gonna come in or what?" Kekoa shouted from across the yard.

She opened the gate for Tenn and they walked over to the carport, where the family was already tearing into the bags that he'd brought.

"You all *pau* or is there more work I can help with?"

"There's always more work," Kekoa said. "We're done with the roof on the main house, but the roof blew off the chicken coop."

"The roof blew off a long time ago," Lani said, "it wasn't

this little storm. Anyway, the chickens don't use it."

"Maybe they would use it if it had a roof," Tenn said with a grin.

Lani narrowed her eyes at him, but his grin didn't falter.

"Can I help?"

"I don't think we even have more roofing to use. Emma's been using it to fix the fence."

"We took all that down," Kekoa said through a mouthful of kalua pork. "We fixed the fences. All that corrugated tin is in a pile just over there."

"Great!" Tenn strode through the carport.

"Great," Lani said flatly. Kekoa laughed at her, and she tossed a french fry at him in passing.

Tenn walked past the pile of metal to go check out the chicken coop. It was in decent shape, lack of a roof notwithstanding. It was newer than any of the other buildings, with special doors on one side where they could reach in and collect eggs. If the chickens ever actually laid there.

It did still have a bit of roofing left, and he was looking it over to see where it attached.

"This should be a quick fix," he told her. "I'll just need the stuff that your family was using to fix the main roof."

Armed with a cordless screwdriver and a box of roof screws, he made quick work of the henhouse. The scrap roofing was rusted through in places, but they overlapped it and managed to patch together a sturdy roof. Lani carried the pieces as Tenn secured them on, telling herself that it was to help him get out of there faster.

"That should do it," he said as he secured the last piece of roofing. "If we clean it out and put some nice bedding in the nest boxes, you should get at least some of the hens going in there to lay. Better yet, you can put them in there at night to sleep."

"Do you have chickens?"

"Not anymore, the restaurant keeps me busy enough. But my parents have always kept chickens."

"How are we supposed to make them sleep in the henhouse? I don't fancy herding chickens every night."

"You can actually pick them up while they're sleeping and move them in. They wake up there and their little dinosaur brains figure it's their new sleep spot."

"Worth a try, I guess."

They walked back around the house and paused, watching Kai and the girls play some elaborate game of tag.

"Will you let me take you to dinner?"

She turned to him in surprise.

The rapid rush of blood in her ears drowned out the stern warnings of her thoughts. She had sworn off men. But this was different.

This was Alfie.

"Olivia will be with my parents tomorrow. Do you like sushi?"

"I love sushi. But..." She trailed off, not wanting to assume. But he wasn't exactly being subtle. "Alfie, I'm not in a position to date anyone right now."

"It doesn't have to be anything more than it is," he replied.

"What does that mean?"

"Just two old friends catching up over sushi."

"I don't think—"

"They have great poke bowls too."

"I'm still married."

His smile fell, but his eyes held hers. "Are you still together?"

"No."

"Is there any chance of you getting back together?"

"Definitely not."

His smile sprang up again, an irrepressible weed. "Then it's a date."

16

Emma

Worms wriggled away, diving for cover as Emma raked her finger through the rich black soil.

She had spent nearly a week of long days clearing out John's old garden beds. They were so overgrown that she never would have known they were there had Mahina not pointed them out. By the end, she had a compost pile the size of a car and a huge garden full of clean soil ready for planting.

With AirBuds in her ears and her phone in her pocket, she called her big sister.

"She lives, she breathes!" Toni answered.

Emma sighed. "Why is everyone in this family so dramatic?"

"We haven't heard from you in months."

"You're ridiculous."

"What?"

"I haven't even been gone *one* month."

"Feels like four."

"This from the woman who spent her formative years pinging between continents like a pinball."

"Well, this is my first time on the other end of it. It sucks. We finally got the whole family together and then you disappear."

Emma was quiet for a moment, tucking sweet potato slips into the freshly turned soil. Finally she said, "Toni, I had to."

Tony was immediately contrite. "I know. I'm sorry. I was just giving you a hard time. We miss you."

"How are you?"

"All's well here. Juniper's amazing, she's been running a stand out at the Wednesday market all on her own. And I can't keep my website stocked; everything keeps selling out." She paused for a moment and then asked, "When are you coming home?"

Emma took her time replying as she found the taro corms Mahina had given her and tucked them into a low spot in the middle of the garden. "I'm thinking about staying for a while."

"Well, I can't blame you for skipping out on winter. The rain has been nonstop." There was a beat of silence. "How long is a while?"

"Indefinitely," she admitted. "Kai is so much happier here. *I'm* so much happier here."

"Then I'm glad that you're there. When can I come visit?"

Emma laughed. "Whenever you like."

"See, that's the benefit of far-flung family that no one ever talks about. Now I have an excuse to visit Hawai'i."

"And a place to stay. I need to put some work into the *'ohana* unit though. It's a literal rats' nest right now."

"Okay, so maybe we can visit after you get that sorted out."

"Dio's on it."

"Who?"

"Our dog." She watched Kai race past with Dio at his heels, the picture of childhood.

"You got a dog? Man, you *are* putting roots down there."

"It wasn't deliberate. We found him." She thought of how the puppy had crept towards their car, hopeful in spite of his fear. "Or he found us, I guess. We can bring him with us when we come back. Whenever that is."

She picked up the cardboard box full of slips and carried it to the end of the row. "You'll never guess what I'm doing right now."

"What?"

"Planting sweet potatoes."

"Ha, I knew it."

"Knew what?"

"That you were a gardener at heart."

"That's what I was calling about, actually."

"And here I thought it was to hear the sound of my voice."

"That too. But I wanted to ask you what I should plant. I got a bunch of sweet potato slips from Adam's family, and that should give us plenty of carbs. And there's lots of fruit growing here. But I want to grow vegetables, and I don't know what will do well here in the tropics. I figure that you would know, that it would be a lot of the same stuff that you used to grow in Costa Rica."

"I'll send you some seeds."

"No, you don't have to do that. I was just hoping that you could recommend–"

"I'll send you some seeds," she said again. "Don't try to argue with me. Seed shopping is my favorite pastime. My personal seed library is too large for me to even consider buying anything new for a year or ten, but I would love the excuse to rack up some purchases. My favorite heirloom seed company ships free, even to Hawai'i. I *do* know what stands a chance in that climate. *And* I know what you like to eat. So. Text me your address, and leave it to me."

"Okay, thank you."

The call disconnected, and she put the earbuds back in her pocket.

She finished planting the cuttings that she had been gifted and stood, looking over the rest of the garden space. There was still so much room for food. She would have to be careful to keep it weeded while she waited for seeds.

"You resurrected John's garden!" Tara called over the fence.

"I'm trying to." Emma wiped sweat from her brow with the back of her arm as she walked across the yard.

"Do you want some starts? I always get overexcited and start way more seeds than I need. I have about a dozen tomato plants outgrowing their pots because I ran out of room in my garden."

"That would be great, thank you."

"Stay right here, I'll go grab them."

She came back a few minutes later with a tray full of tomato plants, each about six inches tall. Emma held the tray carefully, accepting it over the top of the fence.

"Thank you so much."

"I'm just happy to get them in the ground. I need to expand my garden, but the animals keep me so busy I just can't find the time." She looked at the long mounds of clean dirt and the mountain of weeds that she'd removed. "You did a great job."

"I probably should have started with the orchard, but it's so overwhelming. How do I get rid of that cactus grass?"

"You mean the razor grass?"

"I don't know, is that the same thing?"

"Let me take a look."

Tara came around through the gate and they walked together

to the orchard, where Emma pointed out the head-high grass that had filled her palm with fiberglass-like spines.

"Yeah, that's the stuff," Tara said. "Just wear gloves and cut it. Goats love it."

"They eat it? Really?"

"Yeah, goats will even eat blackberry brambles. But this stuff makes great fodder, that's why it was introduced. You could let the goats into the orchard to eat it, but you'll have to stay on top of them to make sure they don't get the fruit trees. I usually just cut and carry it. My cow loves it."

"You have a cow?" Emma exclaimed.

Tara chuckled. "Yeah, you haven't heard her? She's out on the back lot with the sheep. And her baby, of course."

"How do you do it?"

"It never ends, but I love it. I should get back to it. I have about ten more things I want to get done while the girls are at their friend's house."

"Thanks again for the tomatoes."

"Get them in the ground today if you can. They're overdue for a transplant. You know to bury most of the stem, right? Just leave a few inches above ground.

"I'll do that, thanks."

She went back to the garden and set out the gifted starts, giving each tomato plant plenty of room and a tall branch that she could tie it to as it grew. Then she looked all around the garden for her trowel, but she couldn't find it anywhere.

"Kai, have you seen my little hand shovel?" She straightened up and looked around. "Kai?"

She tried again on the walkie talkie, but he didn't respond there either.

The twins were gone for the day, and Rory was off at 'Ōlena's daycare, so it worried her when he didn't respond. She went looking for him and found him in the green fort that the kids had made amongst the bushes and vines. He was holding a small kitchen knife and sat looking down at a dead lizard.

"Kai!" She exclaimed. "What are you doing?"

He started and then stared up at her. "Science."

"What?"

"I wanted to see what was inside."

She stared down in disbelief. He had made a clean incision down the belly and disemboweled the thing. The entrails were all laid out on a big leaf. She was equal parts horrified and impressed.

"Kai, that poor lizard..."

"I didn't hurt it!" he shouted. "I found it! It was already dead. I found it and I wanted to see what was inside. I didn't do anything wrong. You always get mad at me when I didn't do anything wrong!"

He threw the knife down and sprinted off, Dio running cheerfully at his heels. Emma looked back at the gruesome scene and shuddered. She felt deeply disturbed by the gutted lizard, but she also felt sorry for her reaction. Kai could easily grow up to become a surgeon, and here she was scolding him for what was really quite an impressive attempt at an autopsy.

She took refuge on the shade of the front porch and texted Lani.

I can't tell if my son is going to be a brilliant scientist or a serial killer.

Why not both? she replied.

I just found him with a gutted lizard. He had the organs all laid out before him like a soothsayer of old.

Lani started typing several times over before she finally sent,

I've got customers. We're gonna have to untangle that one when I get home.

Fair enough.

A few minutes later, another text came through. *Maybe he'll become a veterinarian.*

Here's hoping.

17

Lani

Tenn pulled up to the house with four surfboards in the back of his truck. He had followed up on their sushi date with gentle insistence, and somehow it had ballooned to include surfing before dinner.

"Is it a double date?" Lani joked as she opened the gate.

"So it *is* a date," he said.

"I mean, are we picking up some other people?"

"I wasn't sure what sort of board you'd want, so I brought all three of my boards and a smaller one of my mom's."

"She still surfs?"

"Not as much as she used to, but yeah."

"Very cool."

"Yeah, she's pretty amazing." His mouth quirked into a crooked smile as he added, "It's almost enough for me to overlook the name she gave me."

"You could always change it."

"No, I'm used to it. It's worn in. Like an old pair of shoes."

"So, where are we going?" she asked as she climbed into the

truck.

He handed her a cold bottle of sugarcane juice. "I was thinking Honoli'i."

She chewed on her lip, looking out the window as they drove slowly through the neighborhood.

"Is that okay?" he asked

"I haven't surfed in... man, close to a decade? I'm worried that he will be too much for me."

"We can go wherever you want. But the surf is mellow today, and I think you'd have fun there. I remember seeing you out on the water in high school. You don't forget a thing like that. Surfing, I mean. It's like riding a bike."

She smiled self-consciously.

"What?" he asked.

"I never learned how to ride a bike."

"For real?" He smiled at her and then turned his eyes back to the road. "Now I know what to do for our second date."

It was a gorgeous day, pale blue skies and dark blue water. The river beneath the bridge was calm and clear. And he had been right, the surf was perfect. Big enough to be fun, but not overwhelming.

Tenn found a parking spot just past the stairs, and Lani chose the smallest board from the back of the truck. It was a pale sunshine yellow, faded with age but still in great shape.

They carried their boards down the hill and across the warm black sand until they reached a spot where it was easy to get in. Lani walked out through the surf, pulled herself onto the board, and started paddling.

Muscle memory kicked in immediately, and she felt a rush of pure joy as she skimmed across the water. Her arms weren't as strong as they used to be, but the old motions were as familiar to her as ever.

There was a crowd of people like always, and for a long time she just sat there on her board, relishing the view and enjoying the gentle bob of the water surging beneath her. She watched as others caught waves and rode them.

Then Tenn lured her into the perfect spot.

"I don't know," she said as a big wave rushed towards them.

"You've got this. Here, take this one!"

She pointed the nose of her board towards shore, looking anxiously over her shoulder.

"Go!" Tenn cheered behind her. "Go! Get it!"

She paddled furiously, shoulders burning. For a second, she thought that the wave would pass underneath her and leave her behind. But she kept up and caught it, board surging up beneath her in a rush of speed as the wave drove her forward.

She lifted her hands out of the water and flew.

The rush of wind and water sent her straight back to her childhood, out there with her dad.

And Tenn was right. It was like she had never been away. She steadied herself with her hands and hopped up onto her feet like it was nothing. The wave took her almost all the way to the rocky shore before she steered herself over the back of it and landed with a gentle splash.

As she paddled back out towards the other surfers, they all clapped and cheered.

Tenn cheered first, last, and loudest of all.

"You can take the surfer girl out of Hawai'i," he said as she paddled back to the line up, "but you can't take Hawai'i out of the girl!"

After a few more waves, she went in. All that paddling had made her muscles ache and burn. She carried the borrowed surfboard up out of the water and set in the warm black sand. Then she plopped down beside it, relishing the afternoon sunshine that warmed her back.

As she watched, Tenn caught a wave and popped up to his feet. The sun glinted off of his golden skin as he carved through the water. Then he lost his footing and landed with a splash.

Lani giggled, feeling younger than she had in years. She lay back and turned her face up to the sun, feeling the heat of it on her lips.

Black sand coated her skin and sparkled in the sunlight. It was filled with tiny pieces of sea glass, sparking like stars in the black. Blue and green and white and gold, all glinting in the sun as she turned her arm this way and that.

When the sun retreated to the far side of the island and shadow overtook the beach, Tenn came in and found her still lounging on the sand. They rinsed off at the showers and changed into dry clothes, and then he drove her into Hilo for dinner.

The sushi place was a small building in a gorgeous location, out on a small peninsula with a wide view of the bay. But the windows were dark, and the parking lot was empty.

"What time does it open?" she asked.

Tenn grinned. "Oh, they're not open today."

She looked at him in confusion, but he was already climbing out of the truck. He circled around and opened her door for her, then led her up the stairs and into the restaurant.

"I worked here for years," he explained as he unlocked the door. "The owner is a good friend of mine. He said it would be okay for me to borrow the place for a few hours."

The place was small and fancy, with a long bar in front of the sushi counter and a series of tables that overlooked the water.

He seated her at the very end of the sushi bar, next to a broad window with a view of the bay. Then he disappeared into the kitchen for a while and reappeared on the opposite side of the counter with his arms full of food.

"Something to drink?"

"Water is fine."

"Sparkling?"

"Sure."

He poured her a glass of bubbly water and added a fresh slice of lemon before getting to work. She watched as he deftly sliced fresh fish into sashimi.

"I'm starved," he said apologetically. "Do you mind if we start with sashimi and seaweed salad?"

"That sounds amazing."

"I can make some rolls after that."

He set the sashimi plate in front of her, then went back into the kitchen.

She looked out over the water. The sky wasn't quite dark, but the lights were starting to come on in Hilo. Across the bay, she could see the steady motion of headlights on the highway.

He came out with two bowls of seaweed salad and joined her at the bar.

She picked up a piece of the sashimi. It was some kind of white fish, almost translucent. A small bowl held chili pepper water, and she dipped the fish in that before bringing it up to her mouth. It was incredibly delicious, fresh and clean, so delicate that it basically melted away. The seaweed salad was a perfect accompaniment, more hearty and savory than the sugary stuff sold at the big chain stores, which was always dyed acid green.

"This is phenomenal," she said between bites. "Did you go

to culinary school?"

"Business school," he said with a flat voice and a wry smile. "But four years of academia was bad enough without following it with a lifetime in an office building. I moved home and worked a few odd jobs before landing here. I started out in the back and graduated to sushi chef eventually."

"And then you bought the café?"

"Less than a year ago, yeah. Late nights here were fine in my twenties. I had the whole day to surf or sleep if I needed to. But once I had Livie full time, I knew that I needed to figure something else out. I ran the café for a year before I actually bought it. My parents helped; they're my not-so-silent investors.

"The café is perfect because I can mostly work while Livie's with ʻŌlena or her grandparents. And if there's a week that things get a bit out of hand and I'm working extra hours, she can just hang out with me in the café or ride along with me to get ingredients. We're not open for dinner, so I'm always home to have dinner with Livie and put her to bed."

"Except for tonight."

"True," he acknowledged. "Tonight she's doing a movie marathon with her grandma."

He scraped his bowl clean and stood.

"Do you have a favorite kind of roll?"

"I like ʻ*ahi*. The spicier the better."

"Spicy ʻ*ahi* roll, coming right up."

When he walked back around to the kitchen, she pulled her phone out to text Emma.

Rory OK?

"Would you like some *sake*?" Tenn asked from behind the sushi bar.

Lani jumped in surprise.

"Sorry. Didn't mean to startle you."

"It's not your fault," she told him. "I startle easy these days."

"So, *sake*?" He held up a small, delicate bottle. "This one is—"

"I don't drink," she said quickly. Her cheeks flushed with embarrassment. "Not since before Rory."

"That's a long time." He stashed the bottle beneath the counter and got to work on the sushi rolls.

"Everybody drank a lot on the cruise ships," she said, and then the rest came tumbling out in a rush. "Every night. And off the ship, between contracts, we would drink even more. It was so normalized that it never occurred to me that I had a problem. But when I got pregnant with Rory, *not* drinking was more difficult than I expected. And when she was a baby, I realized that I felt worlds better without it."

That was all true, or true enough.

What she didn't mention was her fear that if she started again, she would lose control. Between the long, dark days of winter and the extreme isolation of their cabin in the woods, any level of drinking had felt like a slippery slope that she wasn't willing to approach.

She watched it happen with Zeke as six-packs turned to boxes turned to bottles.

It was too easy to get mired there. And she couldn't do that to her daughter.

"Rory's lucky," Tenn said.

Lani looked up with a start. His eyes were on the sushi roller as he pressed their food carefully into shape.

"Olivia's mom drank. Similar thing. Restaurant culture,

drinks after shifts. It seemed normal. Difference is, she didn't stop when Olivia came along. I mean, she did. But not for long."

"How did you meet her?"

"We both worked at a restaurant across town, just before I started working here." He took a breath. "We were already broken up when she told me she was pregnant. She moved in with me after that, and we tried again for a while, but it was no good."

He was quiet for a moment, slicing the roll into even pieces. "Even when Olivia was a baby, her mom wasn't around much. She couldn't keep a job for long.

"By the time Livie was four, her mom was living over in Kona. She'd drive over the occasional Saturday, but that was about it. She never took Livie back with her, and it was just as well. Her boyfriend wasn't..."

Tenn trailed off and handed her a plate of food.

"He was driving, the night that she died. They were both drunk – and then some."

"I'm sorry."

He nodded, eyes down on the next roll. "Mostly I felt like I had dodged a bullet. All I could think about was how Livie could have been in that car. I had been pushing for her mom to step up and take her more, work her way up to half time. Every day I thank God that she didn't, that Livie wasn't there when it happened."

"Alfie-"

"Sorry." He gave her a quick, watery smile. "I didn't mean to– I don't usually talk about that. You go ahead and eat, okay? I just need to grab something from the kitchen."

He disappeared through the swinging doors, and her phone buzzed with a new message.

Rory's fine. She and Kai decided that they're going to sleep in the blanket fort we made in the living room. They're in there now listening to a stories podcast.

"Everything okay at home?" Tenn asked as he came back in.

A small smile pulled at her as she put her phone away. "How did you know?"

"That you were checking on Rory? Because I was doing the same thing." He held up his phone and showed her a picture of his mom and Olivia in matching pajamas.

"She looks just like her," Lani marveled.

"It's a trip, right?" He smiled at the picture and then tucked his phone away.

"Before I moved home, I never left Rory with anyone."

Tenn nodded in understanding. "I get anxious when I don't see her for a while, even if she's with my parents. There's just some caveman part of my brain that I can't convince she's okay when she's not in sight. So my mom sends me photos. Even 'Ōlena sends some." He chuckled. "She thinks I'm a nuisance."

"I'm sure she understands. I mean, we're talking about a woman who started a co-op just so she could be with her girls all day."

Tenn finished making sushi rolls and joined her at the bar again. The spicy ahi roll that he'd made for her was phenomenal. They enjoyed the food without talking much, just eating their fill and looking out at the moonlight that moved across the surface of the bay.

When he went into the kitchen to clean up, refusing any help, she checked her phone again. There was a picture of Rory and Kai, sound asleep in their elaborate blanket fort.

Stay out as long as you'd like, Emma encouraged her.

Lani's ears burned with a blush. There wasn't much nightlife in Hilo, especially for someone who didn't want to step foot in a bar. There wasn't even a movie theater.

Olivia was at her grandparents' house. They weren't... surely Tenn didn't expect...

She shoved her phone back in her purse, willing her blush to fade before he came back out. She never should have agreed to a date. She wasn't ready for this.

"Ready to head home?" Tenn asked as he walked back out. "I'm useless past nine these days, I'm always up so early for work."

"Yeah, perfect," she said quickly. "I want to get home to put Rory to bed."

"For sure." He held the door open for her and locked it behind them. As they walked out to his truck he said, "So. Next time. Up for a bike ride?"

"Sure." She made an effort to keep her voice steady as her heart raced with a confusing mixture of anticipation and anxiety. "Next time."

18

Emma

The Pualena farmers market stretched from the long gravel parking lot all along the sea cliffs. The stands were well back from the cliffs' edge and the waves that sometimes lapped up over them, but the salt mist created by the crash of waves on stone hung heavy in the air.

Lani was helping Kekoa man the shave ice stand that had preceded his more permanent stand in town. He still set it up once a week on Sundays.

Rory hung close to her mom, eating her fill of shave ice with white pineapple syrup.

Kai stuck to Emma like a burr, even more ill at ease out among strangers than she was. Still, they had to try. Farmers markets were less stressful somehow than stores or parties. Anytime she felt overwhelmed, she simply turned to the east, and all she could see was ocean. Even the sound of the crowd was lost in the wide open space and the noise of water on rock.

Adam had been the sociable one, and she had been happy enough to go along. Kai had been social too once. The change in him after Adam's death was so drastic that his grandmother had insisted that Emma take him to therapy.

Maybe her mother was right. Maybe Emma should have found him a therapist months ago. But he was so young. She wasn't convinced that being made to sit in a room with a stranger every week would do him any good.

Probably she was the one who needed the therapist.

She shook her head, trying to step out of that self-imposed isolation in the middle of a crowd. The vendor nearest them was squeezing oranges and adding shots of *liliko'i* juice to each glass. She purchased one and took three big gulps before handing it to Kai, who proceeded to nurse the straw and peer out at the festivities with narrow-eyed suspicion.

At least they had gotten off of the property today. That was a small victory in and of itself.

She recognized a woman from their neighborhood who sold produce at a stand in front of her house every day, a mixture of home-grown fruit and vegetables from island farms. Her Sunday bounty was all that and then some. Emma stocked up on familiar vegetables, like oversized carrots from Waimea, and then pointed to a pile of lumpy root vegetables that she didn't recognize.

"What are these?"

"Yams." Seeing her confusion, the grandmotherly woman smiled and said, "Real yams. The African kind. Not sweet potatoes."

She explained how she cooked them - "Just peel and boil, easy." - and Emma bought two pounds.

Walking down the line, she challenged herself to buy something from each stall. A bag of macnuts here, some fresh cilantro there, a small kabocha squash. Kai perked up when she bought him a tiny container of chocolate ice cream, and they returned their empty plastic cup to the orange juice stand, which collected and washed them each week to reuse the next.

"Can we get shave ice?" Kai asked as he scraped the last bits of chocolate from the bottom of the container.

"Sure. Why not?"

She was rewarded with a grin, and they went to see Lani.

"Kai!" Kekoa greeted him. "Howzit?"

Kai scowled and turned away. Kekoa looked puzzled, but a moment later his attention was diverted to a customer. Lani stepped up and smiled at them.

"What'll it be?"

"Lemonade," Kai said.

"Excellent choice. I made the lemon syrup myself. Emma?"

"I'll have the same."

Eating their shave ice, they ambled towards the end of the line to see the stands they had yet to visit.

At the truck that sold pasture raised chicken and farm fresh eggs, she saw a familiar face. She couldn't remember his name, but she recognized him from her summers on island with Adam. He was just an acquaintance, a friend of a friend of a friend, a surfer who frequented Adam's favorite spots. Her first impulse was to turn and run, but she stood steady.

One thing from every stand.

She braced herself and stepped up to the window.

"Hey, Emma! Long time no see! How you been?"

"I'm doing all right. How are you?"

"Just another day in paradise. This your son?"

"Yes, this is Kai."

"Good name. Nice to meet you, little braddah. You look just like your dad."

Kai scowled and stomped out of sight, just around the corner and into the shade of the truck, where the man couldn't see him from his window. Unfazed, the man grinned and took her order.

"So how long are you here?" he asked as he rang her up.

"I'm not sure yet. Here for a while."

"That's great! Tell Adam I said howzit. I haven't seen him for years. Hopefully we'll see him down in the surf."

She was still for a minute, hesitant to correct him. For a long moment she thought that she would let it be, that beautiful thought that Adam would show up in the lineup some sunny day.

Then she thought of coming to the farmers market next week and having this friendly stranger call out and ask after her husband.

And the week after that.

And the week after that.

As if she needed one more reason to act like a hermit.

"He died," she said softly as she accepted the chicken she had purchased. "A few months ago."

The man put his hand over hers, and it caught her off guard. She was surprised by how much that small gesture of compassion touched her. This island loved Adam nearly as much as she did.

"He was a good guy. " He lifted his hand from hers and put a dozen eggs on top of the chicken that she had purchased. Then he added a container of cream cheese. "I never saw him lose his temper. He never snapped at nobody."

"He was the best," she said simply. Talking about her husband in the past tense was horribly painful. But not talking about him was worse. "Thank you so much."

"See you next week."

"Yeah." Emma smiled. It was thin-lipped and stiff, but she gave herself an A for effort. "See you."

She walked to the next stand and Kai followed, dragging his feet.

There was a table at the very end piled high with shining globes so dark purple that they were nearly black.

Emma's hand flew to her mouth and she blinked back a sudden sting of tears. She hadn't seen these fruits in years. They were fairly common on island but only good fresh, and she never saw them for sale in the stores or even at the farmers markets.

"Kai, look at these."

"What are they?"

"Jaboticaba."

"Jaboooty what?"

She laughed. "Jaboticaba. It was your dad's favorite fruit. Whenever we were on island, he would ask around and we would end up going to some cousin's house, or the neighbor of a friend. And he would just feast on these." She caught the eye of the woman running the stand and asked, "Can he try one?"

"Of course. Help yourself."

Emma plucked a perfect sphere off the top of the pile and handed it to her son.

"Do I have to peel it?" he asked, turning the fruit over in his hand. It was about the size of a golf ball.

"You can, but you don't have to. Your dad used to pop the whole thing into his mouth. Just take a bite."

He took a tentative nibble, barely piercing the thick skin, but it was enough for the juice to rush out into his mouth. He slurped out the insides, and Emma could smell the concord-jam sweetness of it. A moment later, there was nothing left but the seed and skin.

"Can I have another one?" he asked.

"Of course."

Emma bought pounds and pounds of jaboticaba, figuring that whatever they didn't eat fresh, they could use to make juice or jam. She was already so loaded down that she made Kai carry the bag. With her market basket and backpack both full to the brim, they carried their bounty back to the car.

She drove home and put away the groceries, and then they ate their fill of jaboticaba and festive, spiky red rambutan. By the time they had tossed all the peels in the compost pile and washed the sticky juice from their hands and faces, Lani and Rory were home from the market.

"What do you have planned for today?" Lani asked.

Emma wrinkled her nose. "The market was my big outing for the week."

"Grocery shopping does not count as an outing."

She shrugged. "Agree to disagree."

"There's plenty of daylight left. Come down to the hot ponds with me."

That got her attention. "Oh, wow. I haven't been there in ages. Haven't even thought about that in years. Didn't that eruption a few years back destroy the ponds? I remember Adam saying something about that when it was all over the news."

"It erased some, but it also made new ones. Remember snorkling at Pohoiki?"

"Yeah." A bittersweet memory flashed through her mind: Adam in all his snorkel gear, grinning like a kid under the bright Hawaiian sun.

"Well the coral's gone. The lava flow went through there

back in eighteen."

"Oh wow." She thought back to the 2018 eruption that had devastated Puna when Kai was a baby, just months after the only trip they had made to the island as a family of three.

The lava flow hadn't touched Pualena, but hundreds and hundreds of homes just a few miles south of town were destroyed. She tried to picture the area in her mind, those pre-baby days exploring the island with Adam.

"There was already a warm pond there, wasn't there? Back in the trees."

"Yeah, but now there are like five. There's a huge warm pool by the old boat ramp - which is nowhere near the ocean anymore - and then some hotter ones off to either side. 'Ōlena takes her girls there all the time, they love it."

Emma nodded. "Yeah, okay. Let's go."

"Sweet. I'll just put that hibiscus tea I made into bottles. Would you pack some snacks for the kids?"

"Definitely."

There was a comforting rhythm in getting ready to go with someone else, sharing the mental load of making sure that they had everything they needed for an outing with the kids. Kai seemed to feel it too; he was always more willing to get in the car when they went as a group as opposed to Emma halfheartedly trying to coax or command him to leave the house.

Lani drove them south in John's old truck, and Emma marveled at the broad expanses of black lava rock where there used to be green jungle, farms, and houses. The fresh rock curved and sloped, a picture of frozen motion. Some old structures could still be seen peeking up out of the black. Others stood untouched just a few feet from the fresh rock created by the molton flood that had taken their neighbors' homes.

She felt for them, both the destroyed homes and the narrow escapes. They both resonated with her deeply. She and her family had evacuated their homes just a few months ago when a wildfire blazed past their town. Nearly all of the houses had survived. Adam hadn't.

How insane, she thought in retrospect, *trying to contain a wildfire.* To place oneself in front of a towering wall of fire and try to command it.

No one stood in place and tried to stop lava or a tidal wave. What hubris for humans to think that they could stop any natural disaster, creatures standing against an act of God.

She hated herself for letting him go, even in the same moment that logical side told her she couldn't have stopped him. Surely she could have done something.

That way lies madness.

She took a deep breath and turned up the kids' music.

Five years had passed since this particular disaster, Kilauea's grand effort to extend the island's coastline. The road that stretched out ahead of them was freshly paved and there were bits of green everywhere, thousands of ferns colonizing new land.

The kids spilled out of the car the moment Lani parked, and the moms hurried to catch up. The main pond was just steps from the parking area. Water lapped up against the old boat ramp as kids splashed and played.

It was an overcast, misty sort of winter day, and the warm water was a welcome contrast to the cool breeze that blew off the ocean.

Rory flung herself into the warm pool with abandon and swam submerged like a fish before popping up again with a grin. Kai approached more cautiously, taking small steps down the ramp like an old man.

"Mom!" he shouted as soon as his feet were in. "Mom, it's warm!"

"That's why it's called a warm pond," Rory told him. She managed to roll her eyes while treading water, which Emma thought was pretty impressive for four. Kai was two years older and while he could kind of sort of tread water, he tended to look like he was drowning while doing it.

She walked along the edge of the pond, looking out across the fresh coastline. It was bizarre to see acres of black rock where there had once been a protected bay full of clear blue water. She couldn't even see the ocean from where she stood. And the spot where she stood had *been* ocean just a few years before.

"Okay if I go have a look at the new beach?" she asked Lani.

"Of course. Rory's a fish. I'm fine with two."

"Thanks."

"Go take a soak while you're at it. There's one over that way to the left, but I like the one back in the trees the best. It's even hotter than it used to be, like jacuzzi hot. Too hot for the kids."

"Do you want to go first?"

"No, you go ahead. I'll walk over when you get back. We have plenty of time."

"Okay, thanks."

Emma hiked over the uneven ground of the island's new coastline until she reached the beach. It was enormous. Where there had once been clear, shallow water with plentiful coral and tropical fish, there was now a broad expanse of jet-black sand.

The waves crashing against the sand were vicious, and she

was glad that the kids were back in calm water of the pond.

It felt strangely comforting, standing on such a changeable piece of land. This island was always flexing, always growing. It was a living thing, never static. The change could be violent, even devastating, but the island itself was more or less unchanged for all of that.

She stayed out there for a long time, walking barefoot along the black sand. Her breaths came deeper as she let the rough alchemy of it all soak upward, through the soles of her feet and into her bones.

19

Lani

Are you free today? The text from Tenn popped up on her phone just after she got home from dropping Rory off with 'Ōlena for the day.

The shave ice place was closed on Wednesdays. Of course he knew that, owning the restaurant across the street. Maybe he also knew that she usually spent her Wednesdays with the co-op but had been relieved today by a couple who wanted to do a special art project with the kids. It was rare that she did anything both away from work and away from Rory.

She texted back a tentative *Yes.*

Ever been to Kehena?

Lani searched her memory. The name was familiar, some beach down in Puna, but it had never been one of her regular haunts. She couldn't remember if she had ever actually been there or not. Before she could reply, another text came through.

Come swimming with me.

"What are you smiling about?" Emma asked. She set her milk bucket on the kitchen counter and began the process of straining the goat's milk into chilled half-gallon jars.

"Tenn wants to take me swimming."

"You should go."

"You think? I feel weird, going out with him when I've barely gotten the ball rolling on my divorce."

"Not that again. Don't let yourself get stuck in the mud. You like him, I can tell."

"I do like him," she admitted.

"I like him too. He reminds me of Adam."

"Really?" Lani wrinkled her nose. Adam had been a brother to her, and so the comparison between him and a prospective date was off-putting.

"He doesn't look like him," she acknowledged, "doesn't even really act like him. It's something I can't really put words to. His energy, maybe? I think it's that he's just... deep-down good."

Lani's phone buzzed again.

Pick you up in ten minutes?

She gave the message a thumbs up.

Nine minutes later, Tenn was parked out by the front gate. She climbed up into the cab of his truck and they drove south through Puna. The road took them almost all the way to the coast, and then he turned right.

The tiny parking lot was full, but he found a roadside spot for his truck, cozied up against the jungle trees. Lani climbed out of the truck and walked through the trees to the top of the gently sloping cliffs. They were even higher than the ones near Pualena, but down at the base of them she could see a small black-sand beach in a sheltered cove.

"That's Kehena?" she asked as Tenn came up beside her.

"Yes ma'am. It's a bit of a trek down. Let me carry your stuff so you have both your hands."

He stuffed her towel and water bottle into a huge beach bag and then led her down a narrow, winding path through the jungle. It took them along the cliffs for a moment before veering suddenly off the edge.

The trail spilled down the cliff like a waterfall, leveling out in places only to plunge three or four feet down steep, uneven rock. Tenn went first and turned back at each uneven spot to offer her a hand. And she took it, every time. With anyone else she probably would have refused, just crab walked or turned around and used both of her hands for climbing. But she liked having an excuse to take his hand, liked the feeling of her hand in his.

Down at the bottom, it was a straight drop from a cliff her height down to the sand. Tenn jumped down and landed lightly, sinking into the sand and bending his knees. Then he turned and held both hands out to her.

"Jump!"

She did, without thinking. His hands caught her waist and slowed her fall just enough that her feet landed softly in the fine black sand. As soon as her feet were planted, he lifted his hands off of her waist and stepped back.

"You've really never been here?" he asked.

"Never." She looked around, taking in the vivid colors of the small cove. It was so drastically different from the white sand and turquoise water that people flocked to in Kona. Here the entire beach was dark black, turning the water beyond an intense shade of blue.

The black sand absorbed the sunlight instead of reflecting it, giving the whole place a calmer atmosphere than other beaches with their blinding light. The cliffs were black too, punctuated with vivid green of plants that had managed to gain a foothold on the steep slopes.

They walked along the beach, feet sinking into the soft sand, and a small crowd up ahead made her blink and look again. There were about half a dozen elders, every one of them as naked as the day they were born. They stood near the surf, casually chatting and looking out at the water.

"Alfie!" She turned to him and pressed her hands to her face. "Is this a nude beach?"

"Legally? No." His mouth quirked into a crooked smile as a young couple ran past them and into the rough surf. "I heard that cops were handing out tickets not too long ago, but that doesn't seem to have discouraged people much."

She looked back at the elders at the far end of the beach. "I'm impressed they made it all the way down there. That trail was no joke." She turned back to him with a frown. "But why Kehena?"

"It's beautiful, isn't it?"

She took a deep breath and looked out over the jet-black sand and deep blue water. "Well, yeah."

"I'll keep my suit on," Tenn said lightly. "Scout's honor."

She made a noncommittal sound, keeping her eyes on the crashing waves.

"Come on, let's find a spot in the shade. The sand gets burning hot."

They found a nice big piece of driftwood with a bit of shade, and Tenn set down the big bag he'd carried down. They sat shoulder to shoulder for a while, enjoying the beautiful day. Then, suddenly, Tenn put a hand on her knee and pointed out towards the horizon.

"There! See that?"

She followed his finger and frowned, not seeing anything but the bright sparkle of sunlight on dark blue water.

Then a thin gray shape burst out and flew through the air. It rotated rapidly, three or four complete spins, before landing with a splash. Another shape leapt from the water nearby, and another.

Spinner dolphins.

They were so far out that she could hardly see the spray of water when they came up for air, but their playful leaps through the air were easy to spot. The younger ones barely managed one spin before splashing back down, but some of the bigger ones executed an astonishing number of corkscrew spins as they flew through the air.

"That's why we're here." Tenn bumped his shoulder into hers. "They're here most mornings. I didn't want to tell you, in case they didn't show. Either way, really. I wanted it to be a surprise."

"It's a good surprise."

"Yeah?"

"Yeah." She watched with a twinge of envy as a slender, silver-haired woman in a long-sleeve bathing suit dove off the rocks and swam towards the dolphins. Lani was wearing her own suit, a simple one-piece, but she hadn't swam any real distance in ages. Going all the way out to the dolphins without fins or a board was daunting. And with no mask...

She sighed, watching them jump. This was good too. Maybe next time she would bring her gear. She would need to buy some first.

Tenn pulled things from his beach bag, putting her towel and water bottle by her feet. Then, from the recesses of the oversized bag, he pulled two sets of masks and snorkels.

Lani gasped.

"Another good surprise?" he asked.

"Yes!" She snatched the smaller mask and pulled it on, then off again to fiddle with the straps. It might take ages, but she could swim that far. She had to get a better look.

"And this?" He pulled out a huge pair of fins, dropped them in the sand, and then pulled an adjustable pair of women's fins from the bottom of the bag. "Good surprise?"

"The best!" She took the fins and hugged them to her chest.

Tenn's grin was more dazzling than the sparkling water. But this time, she didn't look away. He was the one to break eye contact, still grinning as he looked down at his own mask and fixed the snorkel that was trying to escape its bindings.

With fins on their feet, the swim out to the mouth of the bay was easy enough. The sea floor dropped away drastically, dark and deep, and they swam on.

They paused when they neared the pod, giving the animals plenty of space. Lani kicked her feet soft and slow, just enough to stay at the surface. She breathed through the snorkel and watched dolphins swimming far below, swift and graceful and blue with distance.

Then the dolphins came to them.

Playful and curious, the nearest dolphins swam directly under them. Another pair, a mother and calf, swam past deep beneath the water. Another swam towards them at full speed and jumped, spinning overhead to land on the other side with a dramatic splash.

Lani dove beneath the surface of the water and kicked hard, racing dolphins who could swim ten times faster than she ever would. They swam over and under her, playful as children.

Joy filled her chest, so unfamiliar in its ferocity that she thought she might cry. She couldn't remember the last time she had felt such childlike wonder, completely immersed in this moment in time.

Nearly all of them were bigger than Lani, and the largest ones must have been seven feet long. The longer they stayed there, the closer the dolphins came. Some swam past so close by that she could have reached out and touched them.

A flash of color caught her eye, a trailing length of red, and for a moment she thought that one of the dolphins was terribly injured. But when she turned and looked more closely, she realized that the dolphin was trailing something on its fin. It looked like a long red scarf.

As she watched, the scarf slipped off of its fin and hung suspended in the water for a moment before another dolphin caught it on its pectoral flipper. It made her think of a little girl running with a length of ribbon.

They watched for a long time as the dolphins played catch with the red scarf, passing it back and forth. Eventually, one of them returned it to the woman with long silver hair.

They stayed out with the dolphins for hours, until her legs ached and her stomach rumbled, and then they swam back to shore. She crawled onto the semi-solid ground and turned over in the sand, prying the fins off of her feet so that she could stand and walk.

Tenn sat beside her, already holding his fins in one hand.

"Short of holding my newborn baby and looking up at the Northern Lights," she said, still panting from the effort of swimming back to shore, "that's the most extraordinary thing I've ever experienced in all my life."

"So you want to come swimming with me again?"

She laughed. "Sure."

"Good." He stood and extended a hand to help her to her feet. "I don't come as often as I'd like. I've been wanting to bring Olivia out with me."

"No!" Her legs wobbled and shook as they walked back up the beach to the hunk of driftwood where they had left their stuff. "How?"

"A paddleboard would be best, but getting it down to the beach would be tough. I've been thinking of getting one of those inflatable paddleboards so I could blow it up down here. We could put life vests on the girls and take them out on the board."

She looked over her shoulder at the crashing waves. "Just getting them past the surf would be rough."

"It's not always this crazy. We could go on a calmer day."

"That would be amazing. Rory loves dolphins."

"Olivia too."

Lani gulped all of her water in one go and then wished that she had brought more.

"If I had any idea how long we'd be out there for, I would have brought tea and snacks."

"I should have brought more water." Tenn stood and stretched. "You kick back and relax. I'll go buy us a couple of coconuts."

"You're going to climb down with two coconuts? How?"

He chuckled. "I'll manage. It's not that steep."

"It's pretty steep." She slumped back against the warm sand. "I'd come and help you, but after that swim, I don't know how I'm going to make it up to the car, much less climb up there twice."

Tenn smiled and said, "I'll be back in a few minutes."

She watched him go, feeling lighter than she had in years.

Once he had climbed out of sight, she pulled her phone out of her discarded shorts to check the time and her messages. Nothing from ʻŌlena, and they still had a couple of hours before they needed to pick up the girls.

There was a red notification on her emails, and she opened it automatically. Her mind and heart were still out with the dolphins, and it took a minute for the text on the screen to sink in.

An email from Zeke's lawyer.

She took deep breaths and reminded herself that she had been expecting this. She had filed for divorce on her last day in Alaska, and it was past time for a reply. Breathing slowly, she sorted through the attached documents full of legal jargon.

He denied all claims of abuse. She had expected as much.

All the same, her blood pressure climbed as she read on. He had never struck her, the document claimed. Never punched holes in the walls or smashed a glass vase on the kitchen tiles while she stood there barefoot. And fool that she was, she had no proof of any of it.

Near the bottom of the document, there was a checked box next to the words *Sole Decision-making*.

She stared at it for a long time, her mind empty with shock. At the same time, her heart thumped so hard that her vision went black around the edges.

He was suing for full custody.

He was trying to take her daughter from her.

Slowly, her shock gave way to a steely resolve. She would never let that happen.

20

Emma

"I miss my mama," Rory said mournfully. She was on the floor, half draped over the dog. Dio's tail thumped uncertainly, and he turned his head around to lick her hand.

"Do you want to color?" Emma asked.

"No." She let out a sad little sigh and lay her head on Dio's fur.

Lani had gone into work last minute to cover for someone who normally worked Saturdays, and Rory had been devastated to hear that her mom was leaving again, on a day they were supposed to be together. She'd screamed and wept and Lani had been uncharacteristically frazzled. She'd tried to comfort, cajole, bribe - and eventually just had to pry Rory's hands from her shirt and run out the door.

"I want to go to work too," Rory said.

"Me too!" Kai ran in to the the living room. "Let's get shave ice!"

"Yeah!" She jumped to her feet and so did the dog, barking

and bouncing with excitement.

"We can get shave ice at the end of the day," Emma said. They would go at the very end of the workday so that there wouldn't be a big scene when Rory had to leave her mom again. Worst case scenario, they could stay and help her close up.

"Why not now?" Kai asked.

"At the end of the day," she repeated, and Rory collapsed to the floor in despair.

Dio whined and nudged her with his nose. Then he started licking her face, which set off a fit of giggles.

"Can I watch YouTube?" Kai asked.

Emma took a fortifying breath. "How about the park?"

"Fine," Kai said in the tone that one might expect for a trip to the dentist.

"Rory, are you up for a trip to the park?"

"Okay," she sighed.

"Great." Feeling about as excited as the kids, she went into the kitchen to pack some snacks.

The kids perked up as soon as they got to the playground, joining in on whatever game that the other kids at the park had going. Emma sat watching them laugh and run, but anxiety tainted her joy.

Going into town always reminded her how not-okay she really was.

When she was working in the garden or clearing cactus grass, she felt fine. Her body was busy with something that was both novel and physically challenging, and her mind settled into a temporary peace. If she worked hard enough during the day, she even slept well at night.

Getting out into nature worked too. She hadn't mustered up the courage to swim in the ocean or get out on a hike – too much time alone with her thoughts – but adventuring with the kids was okay. She was always up for visiting a new nature spot with Lani.

But Pualena? Hilo? No thank you.

Quiet as those places were, it was still too many people. And Kona? Forget about it.

Roadside produce stands were okay, but even going to the grocery store felt like a trial. Crowded restaurants made her skin crawl. She had gone to the library once to get a card, and since then she just ordered stacks of books online and picked them up at the front desk, in and out.

Out in the world, she still felt like half a person, anxious and off balance.

Sitting on the park bench, she resisted the urge to escape herself by pulling out her phone. Scrolling through clips and pictures online was an easy time suck, but it was one that never left her feeling any better. She tried sitting with her feelings, being present with herself.

She'd rather cut cactus grass bare handed.

When the other families started to trickle home, she followed through on her promise of a treat. They drove the short distance to Haumona Shave Ice, a charming little wooden building with seating out front.

Rory practically climbed through the front window in her excitement at seeing her mother. Luckily she was equally exited – and distracted – by the prospect of shave ice.

"Can I have strawberry and blueberry?" Kai asked.

"Sure thing." Lani gave him a wan smile. She looked exhausted.

"I want a rainbow!" Rory said.

"You can only choose two flavors," Kai told her, pointing to the sign.

"*My* mama will make me a rainbow."

"Let me see," Lani mused, looking over the bottles of syrup. "Strawberry, mango, lemon, lime, blueberry... I think I can do a rainbow."

"Can I have one too?" Kai asked.

"Yep. Emma, you want a rainbow too?"

"I'll take *liliko'i* and soursop. And ginger, if you want to bend the rules for me too."

"Good combo. You want ice cream?"

"No thanks."

"I want ice cream!" Rory jumped up and down. "I want vanilla!"

"Okay, baby. Kai?"

"No thanks." He wrinkled his nose. He and Emma both loved the homemade syrups over ice, but they'd yet to get on board with mixing shave ice and ice cream like the locals did.

"I want this table," Rory shouted, running over to lay claim to one of the picnic tables.

"How are you doing?" Emma asked Lani as she stepped up to pay.

"One of those days. You?"

"Same."

"Thanks for watching Rory."

"Anytime."

Kai devoured his shave ice in a flash while Rory took her time, taking tiny bites and trying to eat each flavor separately. He watched her for a minute with evident frustration before wandering over to the edge of the parking lot to kick rocks.

"Not towards the cars," Emma told him.

"I know!"

She sighed and took another bite of her shave ice. The flavors were bright enough to cut through the haze of the day. The *liliko'i* was tart and flavorful, almost overwhelming the mellow sweetness of the soursop. Lani had drizzled both sides liberally with ginger, and it all came together beautifully.

"Mom?" Kai called to her from over by the dumpsters. He was pulling at pieces of cardboard, scattering them everywhere.

"Kai, stay out of the trash!"

"Mom, I hear something!" His voice was urgent.

Emma stood and walked over, but all she could hear was the scraping of cardboard as he continued scattering the boxes that had been stacked by the side of the building.

"Stop." She put a hand on his arm, but he shook her off.

"I can't," he said, frantic now.

"Just wait a second, let me listen."

He dropped a box and paused, looking up at her face. She strained to hear and there it was, faint as could be: the distinctive cries of very young kittens.

"Oh no." She looked over to the window that Lani worked out of, but she was busy with a big family of tourists.

"Is it kittens?" Kai asked.

"Sounds like it. Okay." She grabbed one of the bigger boxes and moved it aside. "Carefully. Go slow."

The cries grew louder, partially because they were moving layers aside and probably also because the kittens could hear them. At the very bottom of the pile, she found an old cardboard filing box with a lid.

She lifted the top off, and there they were. Five young kittens crying in distress. One tiny white runt, one fuzzy black kitten, two black with white markings, and one striped orange kitten who bared his tiny teeth and hissed at her.

Any one of them was small enough to stand on her outstretched hand.

Their squeaking screams were made all the more pathetic by their appearance. They were half starved and scraggly, with goopy eyes. The smallest kitten's eyes were completely crusted shut.

"What's wrong with them?" Kai asked.

"They're sick," she told him.

"Can we help them?"

"I guess we have to." She didn't suppose that the overcrowded shelters on the island were any friendlier to ragged kittens than they were to stray dogs.

"How?" The kittens were so visibly ill that even Kai looked daunted.

"With lots of love. And medicine. And a flea bath," she added as she watched fat, shiny bugs leap from one kitten to another.

Rory ran up and gasped loudly. "Babies! Can we keep them?"

"For a little while."

"Can I hold one?" She reached a hand in, then paused when the orange one hissed again, ferocious as a lion and lighter than a golf ball.

"Not just yet." Emma moved the box to a chair and set the top back on slightly askew. "They're very sick, and very scared. I'm going to call the vet that helped us with Dio and see if they can make time for us today."

"Okay."

She glanced at the line of people waiting for shave ice. "I know that I said we could wait until your mom got off work, but we might have to leave sooner to go to the vet before they close."

"That's okay. I want to go with the kittens."

"Mama," Kai asked very quietly, "are they going to die?"

She looked into his beautiful dark eyes, and the grief that she carried doubled. The pain of it was almost unbearable. Certainly back home she had turned away from it more than once. But not today. She held his gaze and reached out to touch his hand.

"I don't know. I hope not."

"What can we do?"

"We'll take them to the vet, and then we'll buy some bottles."

"How can I help?"

Emma's eyes pricked with tears as she smiled, touched by the question. She heard the scrape of claws on cardboard and looked over to see two tiny paws clinging to the edge of the box. A small orange face with goopy blue eyes peered out, and she almost laughed.

"You can start by making sure none of them escape."

She dialed the vet and watched Kai gently lift the orange kitten and place it back inside. Silently, she prayed that the kittens weren't too far gone to help.

21

Lani

"How can he sue for custody when he's not even her father?" Lani asked, pacing back and forth through the living room.

"It's not unheard of for a stepparent to win custody of a child, particularly if they've been there from the beginning." The man's voice was low and calm. "You said that you were already living with Ezekial when your daughter was born?"

The room seemed to tilt, and she landed on the sofa with a thump.

After calling several family law attorneys in Alaska only to be told they were too busy or quoted an exorbitant fee, a friend of a friend in Juneau had passed her the number of someone they knew. This attorney, more than old enough to retire but still busy, was willing to work with her remotely. He had also charged her a fraction of what the other lawyers had wanted.

Even with a steep discount, his fee had eaten up nearly all of the savings she had left. She had no idea what she would have done if she had already used that money on rent and a junk car. What would she have done without the last dregs of her savings, without friends and family there to help her get back on her feet?

This is why women stay, she realized with sudden clarity. *This is why women go back.*

"There's no chance that he'll be given full custody," her attorney continued, "and it's extremely unlikely that he'll even be allowed visitation rights. But the judge will hear him out. Your email mentioned domestic violence. Do you have any documentation? Police records?"

"No." Lani struggled to take a breath in.

She felt as if the pit opening beneath her might swallow her whole.

Quickly she stood and walked into the kitchen, searching for something to occupy her hands while her attorney droned on about legal procedures. If she could keep her hands busy, she might actually be able to retain some of what she was saying. As it was, she had basically blacked out for the past minute or two.

"Do I have to appear in person?" she asked as she opened a can of kitten formula.

"No, you don't have to come all that way. We can file a Motion, Affidavit & Order to Appear & Testify By Telephone. Most courts do zoom calls these days, but, well, you know Alaska. I'll appear in court and you can phone in."

She mixed the formula with warm water, testing it on her wrist to make sure it wasn't too hot. The kittens started screaming for attention as soon as she came into view of the box they were housed in. The orange one nearly leapt over the side in his eagerness for food – jumped so high that he caught the edge with his paws – and so she picked him up first.

"So what happens next?" she asked as she sat down with the kitten on her lap. He attacked the bottle with growling ferocity, gnawing more than nursing. He had already chewed the tops off of two other bottles, and he devoured wet food with the same fervor.

"I'll email you a couple of things for you to sign, and then I'll appear in court. All that's likely to happen at the first hearing is the assignment of a second date, as much as six months out if things are as booked as they have been."

"So..." She tried to pull the bottle away from the orange kitten's needle-sharp teeth, but he growled and grabbed onto her hand with his equally sharp claws. She winced and unhooked them from her skin.

"So it's a lot of waiting, basically."

"Right."

"Live your life," he advised. "Try not to worry too much."

"Easy for him to say," Lani muttered after she hung up.

She put the orange kitten back with his siblings and picked up one of the others, a black kitten with white paws. It drank the formula eagerly, though not with the same ferocity as its brother.

"Someone is trying to take my baby away from me," she told the tiny cat. "How can I not worry?"

"Oh!" Emma paused in the doorway and smiled. She had a tiny bottle in her hand. "You beat me to it."

"This one's nearly done," Lani told her, "and only the orange one's eaten."

"Right." She picked up the runt of the litter and sat down next to Lani.

The white kitten looked a million times better than she had a couple days ago. They had cleaned her eyes – when she could open them again, they revealed themselves to be a startling shade of blue – and washed away about a thousand fleas. She was so small she could have slept stretched out on Emma's hand. But she gulped the formula down just as fast as her siblings, like she was eager to make up that lost ground. Her tiny paws kneaded the air and she drank.

"Did you name any of them yet?"

Emma shook her head. After a moment she admitted, "I'm scared to."

Lani looked down at the tiny creature that had fallen asleep in her lap.

"The vet said it's anyone's guess if they'll pull through or not," Emma said quietly.

Lani stood up suddenly, cradling the black kitten in two hands. She felt a surprising rush of anger at Emma's fatalism. It felt too much like giving up.

She put the kitten back in the box and picked up the other black and white one, which was screaming and scraping the side of the box in its eagerness to be fed.

"There you are, Mama!" Rory ran into the room, straight to the box of kittens. "They're awake! Can I feed one?"

"We'll do the feeding," she said firmly, giving this kitten the last of the bottle. "If you're very careful, you can cuddle one. They need lots of love."

"Hi baby," Rory crooned, picking up the fuzzy black kitten. It cried plaintively.

"Would you trade with me?" Emma asked. "That one still needs to eat, and this one's all done."

She deposited the mewling kitten in her auntie's lap and picked up the white one, which was now full and lethargic. With immense tenderness, she put it down to sleep with its siblings.

"It's a cuddle puddle!" she whispered. "Look, they love each other. That's so cute."

"Lani!" Kai shouted from the living room. "Olivia's dad is here!

She looked at Emma in confusion and handed over the kitten she held. Rory raced out ahead of her and ran across the front yard. Tenn stood at the gate, smiling, loose and relaxed in a way that Lani could hardly remember feeling.

"Where's Olivia?" Rory demanded.

"Sorry, Roar. She's with her grandma and grandpa today. You'll see her at the beach tomorrow."

Rory turned and stomped back to the house, scowling fiercely. Then her face lit up, and she turned back. "We have kittens! Tell Olivia that we have kittens."

"Will do."

Rory skipped back into the house and Lani walked cautiously towards the gate. As she approached, she caught sight of a pink cruiser in the back of Tenn's truck.

"You bought me a bike," she said, her voice flat.

"Not exactly. I found this at the transfer station. It was free, just needed a bit of work. I finished fixing it up today and figured I would bring it by."

She opened and closed her mouth a time or two, not sure what to make of such an extravagant gift.

"If you can get away, I have some free time today. There's a big empty lot a few blocks over that would be perfect for learning to ride."

"I don't have a helmet."

"You can wear mine."

"I'd have to ask Emma if she can watch Rory for a bit."

He nodded, looking like he would be content to wait there all day.

She walked slowly back towards the house, feeling pulled four ways at once. Her first instinct was to tell him to buzz off. And if this were anyone else, if it were some guy that she had just met, she would. A polite *Thanks but no thanks*, cold and final.

But this was Tenn. And she didn't know what to make of that.

In a way, she felt as comfortable around him as she did around her cousins. She knew him with a deep sense of certainty, the way that you can only know someone who grew up alongside you. He was thoroughly good, she knew that.

At the same time, she was keenly aware that this man who kept showing up was very different from the thirteen-year-old boy who had carried her through a high school math class that she would have failed otherwise.

But was he really? Height aside, it seemed that Tenn hadn't changed much. He'd always had that sunny confidence and easy-going smile. It just hadn't affected her the same way when they were kids.

She walked into the house and saw Emma closing the door to the room where the kittens were housed. They had been successfully fed and put to bed. The process would start back up again in an hour.

"He brought me a bike."

"Who did?" Emma looked up with a start, pulled from her own thoughts.

"Alfie. Tenn."

"Olivia's dad?"

"Yeah. He wants me to go with him now. To learn how to ride."

Emma smiled, a brighter expression then Lani could remember seeing on her face since their return to Hawai'i. "Go."

"Are you sure?"

"I'm very sure. Kai and Rory just went next door to see their new baby chicks. They'll be over there for a while. And if she comes home while you're still gone, I could just put on a movie. She'll be fine."

Lani ran a hand through her hair, looking out the window. Through a break in the greenery, she could just see Tenn standing patiently by the gate.

"I can't date," she said miserably. "I don't have time for this. I don't have the space in my head, in my heart..."

"That's what he wants. Your ex."

She met Emma's eyes. The certainty that she saw there didn't stop the twisting anxiety in her gut. "You mean my husband?"

"I mean your ex. He wants to punish you. He wants you to be scared."

Lani swallowed and nodded. Those things were true. She couldn't argue with them.

"The legal process is slow," Emma said gently. "It could be a couple of years before you're fully done with this. Don't let him take those years from you."

She put a hand over her mouth, holding back the torrent of emotion that seemed to always be just below the surface these days, a storm roiling beneath her skin. She looked out the window again, standing quiet for a long time.

"Go ride a bike," Emma said gently. "Don't make it into anything more than it is. You deserve to have some fun."

"Okay." Lani pulled on a pair of shoes and ran out the door before she could change her mind.

Emma was right. She had to keep living her life.

When Tenn saw her running towards him with shoes on her feet, his smile was sun-bright.

"Ready?" He handed her a tall, icy bottle filled with liliko'i cane juice. She unscrewed the top and gulped it down, leaving only the core of ice rattling in the bottle. Then she climbed up into the cab of Tenn's truck.

"Ready."

22

Emma

It was a gray-sky morning, with thick clouds that camouflaged the dawn.

Emma looked out her bedroom window at the misting drizzle, wanting nothing so much as to go back to bed for a week or two.

No good could come of a day that started with a dead kitten... and lately, every day started off just like that. It had gotten to the point that she dreaded opening the bathroom door in the morning.

She didn't know what she was doing wrong.

They had taken the kittens to the vet, cleaned their goopy eyes, dosed them with antiparasitics, and fed them around the clock. She had even borrowed a heating lamp from Tara, the kind used for newly hatched chicks, to make sure the kittens didn't get too cold overnight. They had perked up enough to play and purr.

But despite her best efforts, they kept dying.

One by one, they faded away. Every morning she would wake

to find a new one gone, and the others would mewl pitifully, scratching at the sides of the box and demanding her attention. She had taken the survivors to the vet a second time and paid another three hundred dollars just to be told that there wasn't anything more they could do.

They were so far gone when she found them, the vet tech said helplessly.

She had done everything that she could.

Losing kittens in and of itself was a gut-wrenching thing. But Kai's grief made it a hundred times worse. It was like each small death cracked open the bottomless reservoir of pain and confusion that he had struggled with since losing his dad.

He cried for hours when the first kitten died, the little white one that was even smaller than the others. He wailed when he found his mother burying the second. After that, when he woke in the morning to see the litter reduced by one, he crawled back into bed to cry.

The night before, the fluffy black kitten had been lethargic. She had refused a bottle, and Emma knew in her heart that the tiny cat wouldn't last the night. Still, she had hoped. But she got up before dawn and found her already gone.

The orange kitten was the only one left. He cried so pitifully when left alone that she'd put a sweatshirt on backwards and nestled him into the hanging pouch created by the hood.

He curled up over to her heart and promptly fell asleep, peaceful as a baby in a sling.

She walked outside to bury the latest unfortunate, and that's when she saw her garden.

It was ruined.

She watched in fascination as a huge sow squeezed beneath the fence and a line of adorable black piglets followed her out of the garden. She didn't shout or try to hurry them along. The damage was already done.

The pigs had routed up every bit of sweet potato, every corm of taro.

And her tiny, fragile seedlings were collateral damage.

She'd planted all of the dozens of types of heirloom seeds that Toni had sent in the mail. There had been multiple varieties of collard greens, varicolored tomatoes, cucumbers and flowers and radishes and long beans. Even a rainbow of carrot varieties that were supposed to do well in the heat and humidity of Hawai'i.

Sowing those seeds had been such a comfort to her. Starting something of her own, something new and deliberate.

Kai enjoyed it too, tucking round radish seeds one after another into the earth. And when he inevitably tired of that and ran off trying to catch lizards, Emma stayed in the garden hour after hour, planting every kind of seed that her sister had sent and noting down the varieties and locations in her journal.

Then came the pigs.

Now the garden was nothing more than one great swath of mud. The seedlings had been plowed back into the earth. Even the hardy starts that she'd transplanted had been trampled into the mud.

Emma set down the unmoving kitten and walked into the garden to see if anything could be salvaged from the wreckage.

"Another one?" came a small voice.

She turned to see Rory looking down at the fluffy black kitten.

"Can I help?"

"What?"

"Can I dig the hole?"

Emma opened and closed her mouth for a moment like a

landed fish. "You want to bury the kitten?"

"Yeah."

"Um, okay. You want to use my little garden shovel?"

Rory nodded, and Emma found an old garden trowel. The little girl looked around thoughtfully before walking to a red hibiscus and beginning to dig.

Once she had created a hole of an appropriate size, Rory came back for the kitten. Holding the small thing like a baby doll, she carried it to the grave and put it in.

"Thanks for playing with me, Katara."

"You named them?" Emma knelt down beside her.

"No, Kai did."

Emma very nearly started sobbing, but she managed to hold herself together.

Later, when she was alone, she would weep over the fact that her son had to carry death after death – that he had given each of the kittens a name and she hadn't even known. For the moment, for Rory, she kept an outward appearance of calm.

The orange kitten peeked out of his makeshift sling, and Rory smiled.

"That's Zuko." She looked into Emma's eyes. "Do you want to say goodbye to Katara?"

She looked at the sad little bundle of bones and fur. "Goodbye." Her voice cracked.

Rory put a hand over hers. "In Alaska, we put fish under the plants."

"Yeah?"

"Plants need food too," the girl confided. "But yucky food, like fish guts and goat poop. Now Katara can be flowers."

Emma blinked back tears. "That's beautiful."

"Yeah." Rory shrugged nonchalantly. With the tranquility

of a girl playing in the sand, she filled the hole back in.

"We need to put a stone on top," she remembered.

Rory frowned quizzically. "Like a grave?"

"Um, yes. But a big one."

It was to keep the dog from disinterring the kitten. She had learned that one the hard way.

Rory seemed puzzled by the request, but she was willing to go along with it. She found a likely-looking rock, and Emma carried it over to set it on top of the grave.

"I'd put flowers," Rory said thoughtfully, "but there's already lots. I picked a good spot, huh?"

"You sure did."

"I'm hungry," she announced then. "And mama's sleeping."

Emma patted the top of her head. Her shiny black hair was just like Kai's.

"Let's go make you some breakfast."

23

Lani

"How can he say those things?" Lani paced the yard, too upset to stand still. "It's perjury!"

"It's par for the course." Her attorney's voice was gruff and gentle, both at the same time. "They call it liar's court."

She stumbled to a stop. "What?"

"Family court. It's often referred to as liar's court, because this kind of thing is so common. We'll file your response, and the judge will assume that the truth lies somewhere in between."

"But my response *is* the truth!" She was moving again, grass and gravel shifting underfoot as she paced next to the house. Her eyes stung with anger, but no tears fell.

"I'll file it today," he told her, "and then it's just a whole lot of waiting until the first court date. If you want to change yours at all, you have time. I'm headed into a hearing, and then I can file your response this afternoon."

"Okay." She took an unsteady breath, stuffing down the

many things that she wanted to say. "Thank you."

"Have a good one." The call went dead.

A good what? Lani wondered, looking up at the clear blue sky. It was a gorgeous day, but she didn't feel part of it. The shining green plants and showy hibiscus flowers felt separate from her, like she was seeing them through thick glass.

She hadn't slept at all the night before, but her blood was still so filled with cortisol that she didn't feel the least bit tired. Her whole body vibrated with anger. She started walking again, stomping through the overgrown orchard in an effort to shed some of the excess energy.

Her Alaskan attorney had forwarded her an email the night before, a declaration filed by her soon-to-be ex-husband. Her first time through, she had felt nothing but frozen shock. But then, reading it again and again, she felt a growing anger. She'd channeled that furious energy into her own declaration, refuting each claim point by point.

By the time she finished her response and tried to get some sleep, it was no use. Every line, every lie was burned into her brain.

By sunrise, the whole house was spotless. And Lani's fear-fueled fury still hadn't diminished in the slightest.

"Lani!" Emma called from the lanai. "Tenn's here!"

She cursed under her breath. With all of her energy centered on the brewing court case, she had completely forgotten that she had a date set for today. Her parking-lot lesson had been a success, and they were supposed to bike along the sea cliffs today.

"Tell him I'm dead," she told Emma as she stomped up to the house.

Her roommate just grinned. "Some sun and exercise will do

you good."

"I hate this."

"I hear you."

"I don't know how to live my life like normal while someone is trying to take my baby from me."

Emma walked down the steps so that she stood level with her. "Rory is safe. She's having a great time with her cousins at the beach. He won't win full custody. He doesn't even want to. What he really wants is this. Your stress, your fear. Don't give it to him. Don't let him win."

She slumped down on the porch steps. "I don't know how to live through this."

"And I don't know how to live without Adam," she said quietly, sitting next to her. "But I keep trying. I keep moving. You can too. Honestly, Lani, you haven't even lost anything. You have everything. You just need to keep fighting. Keep living your best life."

Lani curled in on herself, resting her forehead on her knees. Emma rubbed her back.

"If today your best life looks like a long nap, that's okay too."

"No." She thought of Tenn standing by the front gate, all sunny expectation. "I'll go."

"Atta girl."

Tenn had another *liliko'i* cane juice waiting for her in the truck. As soon as she climbed in and twisted the top off of the sweet, nourishing drink, she felt better. The forward motion helped, moving steadily towards the water.

He drove to a section of sea cliffs where the lava rock was broad and smooth.

An established trail wound along the cliffs and through the ironwood trees that grew in clusters. They rode slowly. Lani took deep breaths, relishing the salt tang that filled the air and mixed with the forest scent of the ironwood trees.

The Respondent has a history of emotional problems.

The line from Zeke's declaration came out of nowhere, hitting her like a fist to the stomach. She took in a gulp of air and fought to keep her bike steady.

Respondent should be required to return to Alaska to establish a realistic care pattern for Aurora.

She shook her head, trying to focus on the beautiful day.

The colors were intense, like someone had turned the saturation up on the whole world. Black cliffs, blue sky, green leaves.

Rory is suffering psychological damage, including perhaps permanent abandonment issues, by not seeing her father regularly.

Lani blinked and refocused. The ocean was a deep blue today, closer in color to the dark cliffs than the brilliance of the sky.

The idea that removing a child from the care of one parent can establish a pattern of care by the abducting parent is nonsense.

She focused on Tenn's back as the trail turned into a small copse of trees. Her tires slowed as they moved from smooth stone to a brown blanket of fallen needles.

This game of "Keep Away" is not a basis for maintaining the established care pattern.

The spongy forest floor pulled at her tires and she peddled harder, going just fast enough to keep the bike from toppling to one side.

I have provided and cared for Aurora since before she was born, up until the day she was removed from the state without my permission.

She pushed through the forest, following Tenn through to the sunshine. The day was heating up already, and sweat dripped down from beneath her borrowed helmet. Tenn's dark hair shone in the sunlight.

Respondent has only spent more time with Aurora because she refused to work outside of the home while I provided for our family financially.

She had tried to get a job, had even worked for a few nights as a waitress, but he had gone into a rage and accused her of flirting with a customer.

The Respondent has taken advantage of the finances of me and of others. When she did work it was for less than one month because she had difficulties with her coworkers, which caused her to quit.

Try as she might to focus on the glint of sunshine on water, the blue of the sky, the strong back in front of her, she couldn't stop the litany of lies running on repeat through her mind.

Respondent should not be allowed to decide that I am banned from raising our daughter, which she has effectively done by abducting her to an undisclosed location in Hawai'i.

Her breathing was ragged. From exertion or from stress, she couldn't tell.

Aurora had always been small for her age. When I urged Respondent to supplement with formula when our daughter was an infant, she refused. I fear that Aurora will become further malnourished without proper care.

She turned quickly to avoid a rock, and her front tire skidded out from underneath her. The whole bike went with it, dumping Lani onto a rough patch of ground. She landed on her left arm, and rough lava rock bit through her skin.

"That bastard." She was crying now, really crying. Bright red blood pooled on her elbow, but she hardly felt the burn of the scrape or the gravel stuck in her skin. Zeke's words spiraled through her head over and over again.

So Rory was small. So was she.

Her daughter was vibrantly healthy. She was so smart.

How *dare* he call her malnourished?

"Lani?" Tenn was there, kneeling in front of her, and she got the feeling that he had said her name more than once before she clued in. "Are you okay?"

She shook her head, and more tears spilled out. She couldn't speak. If she tried, she would start sobbing.

"This is all my fault. A parking lot first lesson straight to off roading was too much of a leap. Can I see your arm?"

It was just a skinned elbow, no real damage, but she couldn't find the breath to tell him as much. So she let him take her arm in gentle hands, bending her elbow and wrist with exquisite tenderness to make sure that nothing was broken or sprained. She didn't know what to make of a man who touched her with such care.

She squeezed her eyes shut and buried her face against her knees, embarrassed by her tears. Tenn's hand hung in the air just beyond her shoulder, like he couldn't decide whether to comfort her or leave her be.

"Do you want to walk back?" he asked softly.

"I can't do this." The words rushed from her unbidden, followed by sobs.

"It's okay. We can just walk the bikes back. Whenever you're ready."

"No. This." She picked her head up for a moment and moved her uninjured arm, gesturing between his chest and hers. "I can't do this."

He rocked back on his heels, and a small line appeared between his eyebrows.

"I'm in the middle of a divorce, I'm a single mom, I can't... I just can't. It's too much." Lani hung her head and sobbed.

She unclipped the helmet and let it fall to the ground. The sun shone down on her hair and it drank in the heat, welcome after so many years of weak northern sunshine.

Slowly her sobs subsided. Tenn stayed where he was, quiet. When she finally looked up at him again, he was looking out at the ocean.

"I'm sorry." She wiped the tears from her face and swiped at her nose with the edge of her sleeve.

"Lani, you don't have anything to be sorry for." He turned to look at her, his smile soft and sad. "This doesn't have to be more than it is."

"And what is it?" She sniffed and wiped at her nose again.

Tenn pulled a bandana out of his pocket and handed it to her. "It's whatever you need it to be."

She blew her nose and looked away, out at the endless ocean.

"You don't have to do this alone."

She shut her eyes, suddenly unutterably tired. "I want to go home."

"Okay." He stood and offered her a hand. "Let's get you home."

24

Emma

Emma was astonished to see the sole surviving kitten go nose to nose with their sixty-pound pup.

They fed Diogee mostly raw meat, inexpensive scraps that they bought in huge bags from a rancher with land up in Waimea. He drove his truck full of beef and lamb down to Pualena once a week, and they stocked up on food for themselves and scraps for the dog.

Zuko got plenty of kitten formula out of bottles and piles of canned food, but that didn't stop him from running right up to Diogee's bowl of ground beef.

The pile of food was taller than the tiny kitten and probably ten times heavier, and the dog was big enough to eat him in one bite. But he approached that pile of food with the confidence of a full-grown tiger, growling as he bit off huge mouthfuls.

Dio would back off and stare down at him in shock, then look to the nearest humans for guidance. Receiving none, he would let out a little whine and settle down to wait until Zuko had eaten his fill.

Finally the kitten would wander off, find the nearest pair of human feet, and scream until someone picked him up – at which point he would promptly fall asleep.

He was a spindly little thing, all skin and bones with a distended belly. But his striped orange fur was copper bright, and his eyes were an astonishing color - bright teal, like tropical water.

Aside from getting down for a few minutes a day to play or eat, he wanted to be in contact with some member of his human family at all times. And the humans obliged.

Between pity for the little guy and her terror at finding him dead the next morning, Emma couldn't leave him alone in a box to cry. So she let him sleep with her. His favorite spot to curl up was right against her neck, and she found that tiny ball of warmth surprisingly comforting.

Zuko's will to live astounded her. She herself hadn't really had the will to live for months. Deeply, truly, she had wanted to quit. To follow her husband into the ether. All that had kept her here was a stubborn refusal to orphan her son.

And then along came Zuko. No mother, no siblings. A tiny scrap of orange in a world full of giants. And yet he was so fully, fiercely alive.

The first time that Emma had tried to touch him, he had hissed and spat with all the ferocity of a Tasmanian devil. A wild thing.

Now, every time she picked him up, he purred so loud that his whole body vibrated with it. Such a low, deep sound that she couldn't understand where it came from. He was still small enough to sit comfortably on her outstretched hand, and more fully alive than she had been in a long time.

She wondered if he knew how close he had come to dying.

If he had watched his siblings fail one by one and decided in his fierce little soul that he would not go gentle into that dark night.

Emma had never been a big animal person, never understood how people could get as attached to a dog or a cat as she was to her own flesh-and-blood family. But she was in awe of this little cat. And she knew that losing him now, after seeing him fight so hard to live, would be as gut wrenching as losing an old friend.

And so they doted on him. He was always warm, always fed, never alone.

This one. This kitten would survive.

Belly distended with what would have been less than a bite of food for Diogee, he scrambled over to Emma's feet and stood on top of them, screaming to be lifted up off of the cold kitchen floor. She picked him up and tucked him into the hood of her sweatshirt, which she now always wore backwards for the benefit of the tiny orange tabby.

He purred against her chest as he fell asleep, setting the tone for the day. The vibration moved through her, pushing back the weight of the grief that still weighed heavy on her soul.

It was as if he was recalibrating her whole body to a new frequency set to healing and growth. Pure life.

It was still early, but everyone was already outside. Lani sat out on the back porch with a cup of tea, Kai was on his morning egg hunt, and Rory was picking flowers.

There was an effortless balance of day and night here. She fell into bed just after sunset, deliciously exhausted by a day of labor, and woke at first light.

The sun rose over the water in Pualena, but she'd yet to get down to the cliffs for an unobstructed view of the sunrise. She did make it out to the back porch first thing most mornings, watching the sky over the trees turn pink and orange with the rising sun as hundreds of birds greeted the day.

By the time she got the second goat onto the milking stand, Zuko woke up from his deep sleep and fought his way out of his makeshift sling. She let him down onto the platform where the goat stood, and he opened his mouth to catch streams of fresh milk.

Emma was proud of herself. Just a couple of months ago, she had never milked a goat. Now she was practiced enough to hit that tiny target. And if she missed the first time and got some warm milk in his nose or eyes, well. It was medicinal.

His dangerous respiratory infection was finally gone, and she wondered if the raw milk had helped him to recover when his siblings hadn't. It hurt her heart to think that there might have been one extra thing that made the difference for the other kittens, but she had done her best. They had been so terribly ill when they found them. It felt like a miracle that even one of them had survived.

Once the milk was in the fridge, she handed Zuko off to Kai and headed out to secure the fenceline. Pigs had come through again, rooting up established taro plants and eating young banana trees.

She couldn't hate them, these capable mothers who pushed through the bottoms of fences to find bountiful food for their babies, each of them as adorable as a puppy. Still, they were a menace. If she was going to get any food out of that garden plot, she needed to keep the pigs out.

Eventually, the whole fence would need to be replaced. They would have to take it down a section at a time, put in extra fence posts, stretch the metal fencing tight, and reinforce the bottom with barbed wire. It was exhausting to even consider.

For today, she settled for carting heavy rocks across the property in a wheelbarrow and dumping them at the most vulnerable spots, places where the pigs had already pushed through or it looked like they easily could.

She'd also replaced the screen door with a magnetic screen that Diogee could push through in the hopes that he would still be able to sleep with Kai but run outside if he heard porcine intruders. It meant a whole lot of mud on the kitchen floor and Kai's blankets, but she would tackle that extra bit of cleaning if it meant the dual benefit of her son's comfort and garden security.

She was still hauling rocks when an unfamiliar man showed up at the front gate. Her first response was a gut-kick of fear, wondering if Lani's ex had found them. But this man was older, with silver hair, and his face was pleasant.

"Hello," she said as she approached the gate. "Can I help you?"

"Hi, are you Emma?"

"Yes."

"I'm Liam." He extended his hand over the top of the gate for her to shake. "I'm here about the ducks."

"Oh, Tara's friend!" They had arranged this meetup so long ago that she had forgotten. "Sorry, I lost track of the days. They're all the same here, it's hard to keep track."

"True," he said with a low laugh. "I can come back, if today's no good?"

"Today's fine." She opened the gate. "We'll have to go look for the ducks, though. I'm not sure where they are."

"That's fine." He looked around as they walked through the front yard, past an established *'ulu* tree with huge leaves and dozens of heavy green breadfruits. "Beautiful place you've got here."

"It is. It belonged to my father in law. I'm just trying to keep the animals alive and the jungle from taking over."

"No small task."

"No, but it suits me. More than I thought it would."

They walked back through the orchard, where the trees were thriving.

She had spent a good forty hours that past week cutting back cactus grass and long green vines, carrying it all to the goats and even tossing it over the fence to Tara's animals when she cut more than her own could eat. The sweet cow and her little calf on the back of Tara's lot loved the horrible cane grass, cactus spines and all.

Lani kept bringing cardboard boxes home from work. The idea was to layer them on the ground between trees to suppress some of the weedy growth that threatened to overtake the orchard the moment your back was turned.

In the meantime, the kids were making epic cardboard forts in the carport.

"Here's one." Liam scooped up a large black and white duck with strang red skin all around its eyes and beak. "She's a Muscovy. Beautiful bird. Tame as can be, too."

"Who are you?" Kai demanded. Emma turned to see him standing in a stand of banana trees, holding Zuko to his chest and glaring bleakly at Liam.

"This is Liam." Emma's tone held a gentle warning: *Mind your manners.* "He's a friend of Tara's."

"Why's he here?" Kai asked, belligerent.

"He came to see the ducks."

"Not Freddy!" he cried, stricken.

Oh no, Emma thought. *He named the ducks.*

"Liam has a pond," she said gently. "Remember how happy the ducks were in those big puddles? Wouldn't Freddy love to be able to swim every day?"

"I'll *make* them a pond!" He pressed Zuko into her hands and ran off. A moment later, she saw him frantically digging with a hand shovel at the edge of the orchard.

Liam set Freddy down. "I can come back another day."

"I'm sorry." She sighed and tucked Zuko into his pouch, just now realizing how ridiculous she must have looked when she went to greet him in her oversized backwards hoodie. It had been Adam's, and the sleeves were rolled up and pinned to keep them from swallowing her hands. "It's been a rough year."

"That's okay. You don't have to decide anything today. And if you do decide to make a pond, I could help with that."

"Really?"

"Sure. Not right there," he chuckled, pointing to the spot where Kai was digging, "but you have a few other spots that could work. I've got plenty of fish and water plants to share. You'd just need a liner and some kind of pump."

"I'll think about it. Thank you. I'm sorry you made the trip for nothing."

"Not at all. I'm buying a few rabbits from Tara today."

"She has rabbits?" Emma exclaimed. She'd been living next door for two months now, and every time she thought that she knew the extent of Tara's operation, she was surprised to learn that there was more to it. Carrying feed back to the cows, she passed a menagerie that occupied several hundred square feet of land behind Tara's house; it was home to a pair of macaws that had moved to the island with her decades before. "She's astonishing."

"Agreed." He tipped an imaginary hat and walked towards the front gate. "Give me a call if you want to talk ponds."

"I'll do that, thank you."

Kai ran up to stand in front of her, scowling. His hands were covered in mud, and he had a great streak of mud going up the side of his face.

"Where's Freddy?" he demanded.

Emma sighed. "She's around here somewhere. Liam didn't take any animals."

"Freddy's a girl?"

"Apparently."

"He can't take Freddy."

"He's not taking any ducks today."

"No, he *can't* take Freddy. She has babies."

Emma looked around, but the duck was nowhere in sight. "I didn't see any babies."

"They're still in their eggs. Freddy sits on them all day. Sometimes she leaves to eat and Birdie sits on them."

She was quiet, processing this new information. "Do you think Birdie's the dad?"

Kai shrugged. "I guess."

"I'm sorry that I had someone come look at the ducks without talking to you about it. I didn't realize you cared about them so much."

He was quiet, looking off across. Then he raised his arm and pointed at a large duck with a bright red face. He had a dark gray body and iridescent green wings.

"That's Birdie."

As they watched, the Muscovy duck slurped up a few of the omnipresent slugs that were the bane of her garden, probably an even bigger problem than the pigs. She had tried to start seeds again, and they disappeared as soon as they sprouted.

Birdie found a giant snail hidden in the weeds and gulped it down.

"The ducks can stay," she said.

"And we'll dig them a pond?"

"Maybe. That's a big project, but we can learn more about it. In the meantime, how about a kiddy pool or something?"

"Yeah!"

"Can you be responsible for that? Can you fill it every morning and drain it every night so it doesn't get all yucky and full of mosquitos?"

"I can do it," he said earnestly.

"You know what?" She put an arm around him and pulled him closer, kissing his thick black hair. "I believe you."

25

Lani

"I'm five today, I'm five today! I'm all grown up, I'm five today!" Rory danced around the kitchen, hopping and clapping and shaking her butt to the song that she had been shouting since she woke up.

Lani was working frantically in the kitchen, putting together food platters and party favors. This was Rory's first real birthday party, surrounded by friends and family, and she wanted to get it right.

Whatever that meant.

Her brain was fried by sleepless nights and relentless stress, and the small task of pulling together a kid's birthday party felt gargantuan.

Luckily, she didn't have to do it alone.

"The *piñata*'s ready," Emma whispered. "You bought way more goodies than I could fit into that little unicorn. They're all on my bed, if you want to add them to your bags of party favors."

"The same stuff in both?" Lani's brow pulled into a worried

frown, her default expression lately. "Won't that be disappointing?"

Emma's face quirked into a crooked smile. "How many piñatas have you seen come down?"

"Just the one." She and Rory had seen a birthday party at the park recently. They'd stood and watched as a group of boys dismembered a paper-mache superhero and then fought over his candy innards. Lani had found the whole spectacle somewhat disturbing. But if her girl wanted a unicorn piñata, then by God she would get a unicorn piñata.

"It's a mess. Kai usually ends up in tears because other kids got more or he didn't get the thing he wanted. You can save the day by handing out goodie bags and nipping that jealousy in the bud."

"If you say so." Lani picked up the paper shopping bag full of goodie bags.

She had tried to find things that wouldn't completely destroy everyone's teeth, but the alternative was piles of plastic: bubble wands, stickers, temporary tattoos. Fodder for the Great Pacific Garbage Patch. The whole thing felt like a lose-lose.

"Are you okay?" Emma asked.

She smiled. It felt forced and foreign. "Not really."

Emma squeezed her arm. "You're doing great."

"I'm still standing. That's something."

"That's everything. Why don't you go finish the goody bags? I'll cover up these snack trays and find some room in the fridge."

"Okay, thanks."

'Ōlena and her girls were the first guests to arrive. Mahina and Manō pulled up just a few minutes later, in the same car as Kekoa and his son 'Iolani.

"Where's the birthday girl?" Mahina asked. She made a show of looking around, even though Rory stood just a few feet away with her cousins.

"That's me!" She hopped up and down in her excitement. "It's *my* birthday!"

"Aurora?" Mahina played like she was shocked. "Rory King, is that you? So tall and grown up?"

Rory giggled. "It's *me*, Auntie!"

"So it is! Hello, birthday girl!" She pulled a *lei* out from behind her back and draped it around Rory's neck. "*Hau'oli la hanau.*"

"Wow." Rory lifted the lower edge of the flower necklace with gentle reverence, admiring the spiral of white, purple, and pale green orchids. "It's so beautiful."

"Auntie 'Ōlena has something for you too," Mahina told her.

"This is a *haku lei*," 'Ōlena said, crowning Rory with a ring of green leaves and white flowers that shone against her dark hair.

"I feel like a princess," Rory said, eyes shining.

Lani's own eyes stung with tears. They had missed out on so many years with family, but they were here now. Here in time for Rory's fifth birthday and so many core memories yet to come.

And they weren't going anywhere.

"Quick, take a picture," Mahina said. "While she still has all her flowers."

Rory was happy to pose and grin for one picture after another, twirling in her white cotton dress and smiling wide, showing off all of the baby teeth that she had yet to lose.

They snapped pictures of her with her aunties, with Lani, with her cousins. Even Kai, who generally refused to stand still long enough for a photo and usually scowled when asked to do so, put an arm around Rory's shoulders and gave them a rare gap-toothed grin.

Everyone else arrived shortly thereafter. The little girls from next door came and so did all of the families that were part of 'Ōlena's homeschool co-op.

When Tenn walked in behind Olivia, Lani retreated into the kitchen to rotate a series of frozen pizzas through the oven.

He stood just beyond the kitchen window talking to Manō and Kekoa. He wore a dark green Hawaiian shirt, and his black hair was pulled back. He was so handsome that it hurt to look at him.

So, she told herself harshly, *don't look.*

As she ferried the pizzas out of the house, she was hyper aware of Tenn standing at the edge of things, but she didn't so much as glance his way. She didn't have any energy or attention to spare. Not today.

"Where's the cake?" a small boy demanded when the pizza was gone.

"I don't have a cake," Rory told him, grinning.

"No cake?!" His mouth dropped open, horrified.

"Nope!" She exchanged a secret smile with her mama. "I didn't want one."

"But it's a birthday party." The poor kid looked devastated, close to tears.

"Me and my mama made a special dessert," she said, taking pity on him. She looked at Lani. "Ready, Mama? Can we have dessert now?"

"Of course, baby. Two minutes." She went inside and pulled their tray of homemade pudding cups out of the fridge. Each one got its own candle, at Rory's request. She lit them, creating a spiral of flame around the tray.

As she carried them out, 'Ōlena led everyone in a Hawaiian version of the Happy Birthday song.

Hau'oli la hanau ia 'oe,
Hau'oli la hanau ia 'oe,
Hau'oli la hanau ia Rory,
Hau'oli la hanau ia 'oe!

She blew out every candle, enough for a college student, and everyone clapped and cheered. Then she revealed their grand desert: Cups of Mud. They had made chocolate pudding from scratch, added gummy worms, and topped them off with crumbled brownies. It was a hit.

In some kind of birthday princess miracle, Rory ate two cups without staining her white dress or smushing a single flower.

"It's a perfect birthday," Mahina said quietly, putting an arm around Lani's shoulders. "Congratulations, mama."

Lani leaned into her aunt, so full of grief and gratitude that it seemed her chest might burst. She missed her parents terribly, so much that she had stubbornly refused to think of them all day. Ever since she had moved home, really. It was a black hole of grief that she steered away from again and again, terrified that it would suck her in if she veered too close.

But even with no grandparents, her baby was surrounded by so much love.

Rory was the center of attention at a long table lined with happy, chattering *keiki*. Mahina doted on her just as she did her own grandbabies – maybe even more, making up for lost time. Emma and 'Ōlena had gone out of their way to make this day special. All of these families had shown up for the newest little member of their co-op.

It was a beautiful life, and she felt grateful down to her bones.

After dessert came the unwrapping of presents. Rory grew rich in crayons and coloring books and board games. ʻŌlena's family gave her a microscope, and Olivia gave her a huge marble run set.

Both were forgotten when Rory unwrapped a shiny new garden spade. She held it high and shouted, "A shovel!"

Kekoa looked at Lani. "Who gave her the shovel?"

She looked at Emma, who winced and laughed at the same time.

"It's what she asked for."

He shook his head. "Kids are weird."

Rory was already on to the next present, pulling blue gauze from a big gift bag.

"IT'S THE PRINCESS DRESS!" she screamed, holding a mass of blue tule up over her head. "Paige, it's your princess dress!"

"That was very sweet of you," Tara told her daughter.

"She puts it on every time she comes over." The girl's cheeks were pink. "It's too small for me anyway. I haven't worn it in forever."

Rory already had the costume on over her other dress. Mahina hurried to save the *lei*, lifting it out from between the dresses and draping it over the blue plastic.

The dress was so big on her that she had to gather most of the skirt into her arms to take a step, but she had the biggest smile on her face.

"You might need to put the princess dress away to be able to hit the piñata," Lani told her.

Rory dropped the dress and pressed her hands to her cheeks in a great show of astonishment. "There's a piñata?!"

"There sure is. Should we hang it up?"

"You're the best mom in the whole world!" Rory ran towards

her and tripped on the princess dress. Lani caught her just before she did a faceplant, and Rory launched herself into a hug, crushing the beautiful orchid *lei* between them. "Thank you thank you thank you!"

"You're welcome." Lani pressed her face to the crown of Rory's head, in the center of her wilted white *haka lei*. Her hair was hot from the sunshine, and Lani breathed in the warm smell that had been her home for the past five years. "Ask one of your aunties to help you out of that princess dress, and I'll go get your piñata."

She went to Emma's room and fetched the unicorn that she had stuffed full of lollipops and bits of plastic. Rory cried out with joy when she saw it, and after a five minute deliberation on whether or not she was willing to let the crowd massacre the pink-and-white unicorn, she decided that the bounty inside was worth it.

Lani attached the unicorn to a sturdy nylon rope and tried to throw the other end over the branch of a tree. Her height proved to be an impediment, as usual.

She looked around for Kekoa, but it was Tenn who stepped up and took the coil of rope from her hands. He tossed it easily over the target branch, hoisted the unicorn well above the kids hands, and offered the rope to Lani.

"Would you?" she asked, not quite meeting his eyes.

"Of course."

"Me first!" Rory ran up and stood beneath the unicorn. "Where's my blinefone?"

"You want me to blindfold you?" Lani asked.

Her lower lip came out, and the sides of her mouth pulled down. "At the park they had blinefones. We don't have blinefones?"

"I'll find something," Emma said. She ran into the house and was back a minute later with a bandanna that they folded and tied across Rory's eyes.

Rory spun herself dizzy and staggered to one side, giggling.

Lani handed her a stout stick, and Tenn lowered the piñata so that it was directly behind her. She swung the stick through the air, and the kids nearest to her took several steps back.

The other kids yelled encouragement and instructions and then jumped backwards as she turned to the right and swung again, missing one little boy by scant inches.

His mother yanked him back, and enough people yelled for Rory to turn around that she finally found the unicorn and made contact.

She gave it a great whack before Tenn yanked it up out of reach. She stumbled forward, and he brought it down again behind her. This all kept up until she had given it a few good hits and broken one of its legs, and then the bandanna and stick were transferred to the youngest kid present, a three-year-old girl.

They worked their way up through the ranks, with Tenn keeping the unicorn agile enough that every kid got a chance at hitting it before finally Piper, the girl from next door with short orange hair sticking out from her head in all directions, broke the unicorn open with one good hit.

The children screamed in frenzied joy, and Piper whipped the blindfold off and began cramming her loot into a hasty pouch created by lifting the bottom of her oversized T-shirt.

Emma was right that Kai and some of the other kids ended up in tears when they failed to grab their bubble necklaces or tattoos or whatever it was that they had scrambled towards only to have it snatched up by someone else. And just as she had predicted, Lani was able to restore the peace and staunch their tears by handing out the goody bags.

The wind picked up, blowing fiercely and sending mothers running after candy wrappers and forgotten pieces of plastic. The sky, bright blue most of the day, quickly grew dark with clouds.

"Storm's a comin," Kekoa said lightly, grinning up at the storm clouds.

People headed home after that, looking at their phones and exchanging murmurs of a weather warning. Not quite a hurricane – it was the wrong time of year for that – but close.

'Ōlena stayed to help with cleanup while the girls played with Lani's new marble run and gave each other princess tattoos.

So did Tenn.

He caught Lani alone in the kitchen, and suddenly the day's act of keeping a few yards between them and her eyes on the children wasn't cutting it anymore.

She felt a storm of anger gathering in her chest, directed everywhere but him. She was angry at Zeke for putting her under this stress, angry with herself for not handling it better, angry with the universe in general for presenting her with this wonderful man at the wrong time. It was such a nonsensical storm of feeling that she didn't know what to say to him.

"I wanted to apologize," he told her.

Her chin popped up; his words surprised her into looking him directly in the eyes. Dark brown, almond shaped, deeply kind. There was no anger there, not even resentment or disappointment. She saw nothing but concern.

And something deeper, something that she didn't dare put a name to.

Not now, not with this chaos brewing in her life.

"I didn't mean to push or pressure you," he said softly. "But I think I did, and I'm sorry if I caused you any stress. You just got home, you're still trying to get your feet under you, you're dealing with more than I know. And I overwhelmed you. It was too much too fast."

"You have nothing to apologize for," she told him. "*I'm* sorry."

"Don't be." He took a step forward, and she took an involuntary step back.

It was a dance that she didn't want to be doing, the wrong kind of magnetism. And it didn't make sense, because all that she truly wanted was to move towards this man. He was so good.

She was the one with the baggage. *She* was wrong for *him*.

"I'm sorry that I'm not available right now," she clarified. "I can't be. I just got out of a horrific relationship, I'm at the start of a messy divorce, I haven't even started to grapple with what I'm going to do for work or what my future looks like. I'm a mess, Tenn."

"That's okay," he said. She saw him wanting to move forward, but he stayed where he was and put his hands in his pockets. "I don't need anything from you. Just let me be there for you. As a friend."

She was saved from replying by 'Ōlena, who walked into the kitchen carrying a stack of dirty plastic plates. She looked between Tenn and Lani with narrowed eyes.

Tenn gave them a tight smile and retreated. Lani watched him through the window as he walked outside and picked up the last of the unicorn carnage that blew across the lawn.

"What was that about? 'Ōlena asked.

Lani shrugged and turned away. She didn't have the words.

ʻŌlena dumped the plates into the sink with a clatter. "Girl, you're still married."

"I know that," she snapped. She took a deep breath and grabbed a sponge. "There's nothing... He wants to be my friend."

"Don't try to play tricks on yourself. That man wants more than friendship from you."

Lani scrubbed the dishes aggressively. "You don't think that men and women can be friends?"

ʻŌlena thought about that for a minute. "Men and women can be family. Kekoa has your back. Even Tenn and me, we're a kind of family. He's like a cousin, you know? I've been there for Livie since she was a baby, and my girls call him Uncle."

"Your girls call everyone Uncle," she muttered, scrapping at a bit of stuck-on cheese. That was island culture, saying Uncle and Auntie the way people in other places said Sir or Ma'am.

"Men and women," ʻŌlena continued, ignoring her last comment, "we can be friends in a crowd. It's how we make community for our kids. But you don't see him taking me surfing or making me sushi. What he wants from you isn't friendship. And if you both try to play that it is, someone's going to get hurt. *Both* of you are going to get hurt."

Lani turned her face away and squeezed her eyes shut. If she had been alone at that moment, she would've sunk to her knees and sobbed.

It wasn't just Tenn. It was the cumulation of everything, all of these months and years of stress. And it was so deeply unfair that even after leaving her husband, she wasn't free of him. She was still too frightened, too damaged to open up to this beautiful man.

He deserved better.

"You're right." She made herself open her eyes and look out the window. A duck ran by, trailing fuzzy yellow babies that scrambled to keep up.

That was the only thing she had energy for right now.

That was the only thing that she could be. A mama to her baby.

Keeping her head above water through this oncoming storm was going to be hard enough without inviting extra stress and complication into her life.

The wind picked up to a roar, and trees bent below it.

She went around the house, closing the windows and bracing herself for the storm.

26

Emma

The storm damage was worse this time, yet it didn't hit her as hard. The yard was littered with branches and pieces of rubbish, but the roof had held.

There were no known casualties, so that was something. Of course, there was still time. They had yet to find Freddy and her string of golden ducklings.

She was coming to understand that storm damage was an unavoidable fact of life here. Hurricanes came every year, some worse than others. She had been sure they'd weathered one last night, with the lashing rains and howling winds, but apparently not.

Just a bit of weather.

It was the price they paid for the nightly rain that made this side of the island so lush and green, for the rainbows and sun showers that blessed their days.

She stood at the kitchen window, preparing food for the crowd that was soon to come. Mahina's family had as much land as they did here at the Kealoha place, but they had escaped the storms unscathed, more prepared for them. The day was bright and blue, but the high winds had brought down limbs too close to the house and felled a tree just beyond the neglected *'ohana* unit.

Zuko stirred in his sling and clawed his way out, climbing up the thick cotton fabric to perch on Emma's shoulder, more parrot than kitten. He yowled in her ear, and she set him down by his bowls of food and water. They were up on the counter to keep them away from Dio.

It would take the small cat about a minute to fill his belly and demand to be picked up again. Emma stretched and looked out the window.

The tree had taken down a section of fencing, and Dio was gone. She hadn't thought much of it at first, because he had gotten out so many times before. Generally he explored for a few minutes before looping back around and waiting patiently at the gate for someone to let him in. But he had taken off at dawn before she realized that the fence was down, and three hours later he was still nowhere to be seen.

Kai burst into the kitchen, all frantic worry.

"Mommy, Dio's gone. So's Freddy and her babies, they aren't anywhere."

One problem at a time, she pleaded silently. "Freddy will turn up, sweetheart. But I would have expected Dio to come home by now. He still isn't back? He's not out by the front gate?"

"He isn't anywhere. We have to go find him."

"We will. I just want to be home when Uncle Manō gets here so that we can talk about the work that needs to be done. If Dio hasn't come home by then, we'll go find him."

"We have to find him now," Kai insisted.

She covered the bowl of pasta salad that she had made to feed the family and washed her hands at the kitchen sink. The front gate creaked open and Manō's track rumbled through.

"Here they are now. Give me a few minutes to talk to them, and then we'll go find your dog."

Kai ran to the front gate and stood at the edge of the road, calling for Dio. Worry gnawed at Emma's stomach, a fear that she had been pushing down all morning.

He was right to worry. It wasn't like Dio to stay gone so long. It was horrible to think of him hit and wounded, lying by the side of the road somewhere. She forced the image out of her mind and went to greet Adam's uncle.

"Lani says you have a tree down."

"A big one," she confirmed.

"I brought my chainsaw. We'll get it clear of the fence in no time. Tomorrow we can fix the poles and stretch new fence."

"Thank you so much. I don't suppose you'd let me pay you for your time?"

He just chuckled and shook his head as he went to the back of his truck and lifted out an old chainsaw.

Kekoa climbed out of the passenger side, looking down at his phone. The man had a business to run *and* a young son, and here he was, always showing up for his cousin's widow. The way that family showed up for each other in Hawai'i never failed to astonish her.

She had a similar level of support in California. She could count on her twin brother to show up for her when she really needed him, and her sisters had nearly smothered her with their support following Adams death.

But this was something else entirely, extended family that went beyond blood, community coming together again and again because it was simply what you did for each other.

Kai still stood just beyond the gate, calling for his dog with his hands cupped around his face. His voice warbled and cracked as he stretched it to its limits.

"What are you yelling about?" Piper asked over the fence.

"Dio's gone."

"For how long?"

"All day."

Piper made a face. "It's, like, nine o'clock."

"He's never been gone this long."

"Okay, just a sec. We'll help you look."

"We need a grownup."

"Cody's grown. Or close enough. Be right back."

Tara's son Cody, the elusive teenage boy who lived next-door, followed his sisters through their front gate and over to Kai.

"Your dog get out?"

"He's gotten out lots of times," Kai said. "He always comes back. He's been gone a long time. Something's wrong."

"I'll help you look," Cody offered. "Let's walk up towards town and ask around. Maybe somebody found him and took him inside. Does he have a collar?"

Kai shook his head, and tears spilled down his face. "My mom got him a collar, but it kept getting stuck on sticks in the bushes. It almost choked him, so I took it off."

"I get it. Our farm dogs don't wear collars either. Let's go find him." He looked at Emma. "If that's okay?"

"Yes, thank you. Let me give you my number so you can text me if you find him."

"Okay, I'll just grab my phone and let my mom know."

"You're not coming?" Kai asked his mom.

"I can walk in the opposite direction. You're welcome to

come with me, or you can walk with Cody and the girls."

"I'll go with them," he decided.

"I figured." She smiled and pulled him into a hug. He was so tall now that his head came in just under the sleeping kitten in her backwards hoodie. "We'll find him, sweetheart."

"If you want to go north," Lani said as she walked up, "I can walk towards the water. I'm just going to drop Rory with ʻŌlena, and then I have a couple hours before work."

"Thank you."

Permission granted and phone numbers exchanged, the kids set off in search of Dio.

"Hey Emma," Manō called as he walked over. "We gon go down to Pahoa, but we'll be back later." He put his chainsaw back into his truck.

"We just got a call from a friend of my dad's," Kekoa explained. "They need help clearing a tree. The chainsaw work back there is done. If you clear out around the fence, we can come back tomorrow to move the log and stretch some new fencing."

"Great. Thanks so much."

A call came through to her cellphone as Manō drove off. It was her brother, Ethan. They hadn't talked in ages, so she put the call through to her earbuds as she closed the front gate and set off in search of Dio.

She walked in the opposite direction from the kids, going deeper into the neighborhood while they had headed towards town.

"Hello?" she said as she picked up. "Ethan?"

"Emmaline!" His familiar voice warmed her heart. "How have you been?"

"You want the short answer or the honest one?"

"How about medium?"

"Medium long or medium honest?"

"Ha ha," he said gruffly.

"I'm good. It's a new disaster every day, but they're smallish disasters. Manageable. It keeps me on my toes. I'm out looking for Kai's dog right now, because a tree brought down a section of fencing last night and he went out and got lost. How are you?"

"Everyone's doing good over here. I handed off everything that I had going in Santa Cruz and picked up a couple of remodels here in Redwood Grove, so it's been good. Working less, spending more time with family."

"And how's Laurel?" Emma spoke louder than she normally would, pitching her voice up and out in the hopes that Dio would hear her and come running.

"She's doing great. You should see her, her belly is bigger than it ever was with Juniper. For a minute we thought it would be twins, but it's just one big boy."

He sounded proud and excited, happier than she had heard him in a long time. She had her doubts about his wife and her future sobriety. They all did, after so many years of devastating ups and downs. But all that she could do was hope for the best.

Well, that and be there for them during the overwhelming newborn phase.

"I know that I've been here longer than, well, longer than I expected. But I'll get back there by the time the baby's born."

"Don't worry about it, Em. Live your life. We have plenty of family here."

"Are you sure?" She came within sight of the end of the road and muted herself for a moment to call for Dio. When he didn't appear, she turned and walked back the other way.

"I'm sure," her brother said. "Honestly, I'm not even sure we'll be here that much longer."

"You're not going back to Santa Cruz?" The drug scene there had provided fertile ground for more than one relapse for his wife, and their teenage daughter wanted nothing to do with the place anymore.

"No, not Santa Cruz."

"Where then?"

"We need to get a fresh start somewhere. It's been nice here in Redwood Grove, but we've been talking about going somewhere new."

"Like where?"

"Well... like Hawai'i."

She stumbled into a stop. "You mean it?"

"We haven't decided yet. We've been researching different places. But Laurel loves it there, and Juniper has been talking about the agriculture program there at the University of Hilo. If you're there a while, we'd love to come visit you and check it out."

"Yeah, of course, I'd love that."

"Juniper is in college-level classes." His voice was a mix of bewilderment and pride. "She could get her diploma, or whatever it is, the one kids can test for to get out of high school early. She's already taking classes here at Cabrillo, and then she wants to transfer somewhere else.

"We're ready to follow her wherever she goes. We don't want her to feel like the new baby is replacing her. We want to be a family, even if she's living in college dorms and just coming to us to eat a solid meal and wash her clothes. After all that she's been through, we want to be close enough for her to be able to do that."

"Ethan, that's beautiful. And she definitely wants to come here?"

"There is no definitely with Jun," he said wryly. "But yeah, she's real excited about the permaculture stuff over there, food forests and all that. The kind of stuff that Toni's into."

"This is the place for it," Emma said as she walked through the lush greenery of their neighborhood. She slowed and looked through the fence as she passed the Kealoha place. Freddy ran through the undergrowth, trailed by her ducklings.

"Well I'll talk to my girls about making an exploratory trip out there," he said. "Sometime after the baby's born."

"We'll be here," she said with newfound certainty.

"I'll let you go find that dog of yours."

"Okay. Talk soon."

Emma pocketed her earbuds and walked on through her neighborhood, this tropical place that overflowed with greenery and the smell of growing things.

She would go back to Redwood Grove – probably sooner rather than later, to clear their things out of the house and either rent or sell the place. And although she would probably live there again someday, close to her aging parents, she felt no pull to move back. Not yet.

Adam had lived and died in California, but he was born here, on this island. He had grown up here. And she felt him all around her: in the warm breeze, the smell of the trees, the tropical sunshine.

For now, at least, this place was home.

27

Lani

The road that ran from Pualena down to the coast had no sidewalk.

Lani walked along the thin strip of green that grew between the asphalt road and the fences that marked property lines. In some places it was a neatly cropped stretch of lawn. In others, the weeds were so high that she had to walk around them in the street.

She called periodically for Kai's dog, but she wasn't feeling optimistic. Surely, if nothing was wrong, he would have run home by now.

Diogee never stayed away this long. Occasionally he would sprint off through an empty lot, chasing a mongoose through the trees, but he always showed up panting at the front gate about five minutes later, fifteen at most.

He wouldn't have gone far. Maybe some well-meaning neighbor had taken him in off the street. So she kept calling out. If nothing else, a woman calling for her dog should catch the attention of whoever had him.

She tried not to think of him dead on the side of the road, but she still found herself looking under every bush.

"Lani!" The sudden shout made her jump.

A split second later she recognized Tenn's voice. She caught sight of him down the road, looking better than he had any right to in faded boardshorts and an old Pualena Café t-shirt. He jogged towards her up the side road, and she looked away without really meaning to.

"What are you doing here?" She kept walking, bending slightly to look through the greenery.

"I live here," he said lightly. He pointed down the side street to his truck. "I just dropped Olivia off at the co-op."

"Right." She paused to push a branch aside and peer through the young trees of an empty lot.

"What are you looking for?"

"Kai's dog. Tree took down the fence line, and he got out this morning before we realized. He's gotten out a dozen times before, the fence is so old and slumped. But he always comes right back home. He's been gone for hours this time."

"Can I help you look?"

She looked at him, paused, and nodded sharply before continuing on.

They walked a few more blocks and had nearly reached the ocean before Tenn suggested that they turn down an unpaved side street.

"I don't imagine he would have gone all the way down to the cliffs, at least not without turning right back around. He might've gone down one of the quieter streets. This one has about a dozen dogs tied up outside a couple properties. He might've followed the smell."

"Worth a shot." They walked in silence the length of the

long block, nearly a mile to the next road. When they reached it, they walked back up, another half mile towards town before turning onto the next quiet street and walking in the direction of the Kealoha place.

She kept waiting for Tenn to make conversation, but he didn't.

It wasn't an uncomfortable silence. He seemed content just to walk beside her through the quiet morning sunshine. He didn't try to take her hand – that is, not until they reached a mess of fallen branches.

The storm had torn long limbs from the albizia trees that towered over this stretch of road. There was no going around them, so Tenn clambered over and then extended a hand to Lani. She took it, and he helped her over the mess of the leafy branches.

He released her as soon as she was past it, and her hand ached to take his again.

She denied the urge and walked faster.

In the distance, she heard a whining howl. It sounded like Dio, or at least like some big, young dog. There were plenty of those in the neighborhood, many of them permanently chained in front of their owners houses, so she tried not to get her hopes up.

All the same, her steps quickened to a jog as they approached the source of the noise. Tenn kept pace easily, his long legs eating up the distance as quickly as she could jog.

The sound was coming from a house with dogs chained out front, but neither one of those dogs was making much noise. One flattened its ears against its head and skulked towards its doghouse while the other, not much more than a puppy, whined in greeting and wiggled his whole body as he strained at the end of his chain.

The miserable yelping whine continued from behind the battered wooden house.

Lani took a hesitant step onto the property, following it. The dogs were chained strategically to prevent anyone from crossing the front lawn, but the young one on the right did nothing more than nose her legs in a bid for attention. She patted his head distractedly as she walked towards the side of the house.

Tenn paused at the property line and looked like he might argue, but he kept quiet. She cupped her hands around her mouth and called, "Dio?"

The puppy-like crying intensified to excited whines and yelps, and then she was certain. She turned back to Tenn.

"That's him."

He nodded and walked forward to join her. Standing between her and the porch, he called out, "Aloha! Anybody home?"

When there was no answer, they walked around the side of the house.

Dio was just around back, in a huge metal cage that people used to catch wild pigs. The trap door had shut behind him.

He whined and scrabbled at the bars, tail whipping in excitement. She put her hand against the cage, and he licked her fingers.

"Do you know how to open these?" she asked Tenn.

"Let me see." He knelt to examine the trap door, and just then a shout came from the back of the house. An older man walked out carrying a hunting rifle.

"This is private property!" he shouted.

"This is our dog," she told him, eying the gun.

"If it's on my property, it's my dog," he growled.

"Then we'll get him off your property." Lani's heart was racing wildly, but she kept her voice level. "Would you please open the cage?"

The man spat over the porch railing, a yellow glob of phlegm that landed near her feet.

"What kind of idiots let their dogs run wild? Do you know a lady two streets down was killed by dogs just last month? Not to mention the damage they do to livestock. I ought to have shot him the minute the trap closed."

Lani shrank back, though a part of her wanted to shout right back. Ten years ago, she would have gone toe to toe with anyone. She was never tall, but she was fierce.

She hated this new fear that lived in her bones. She hated what those years with Zeke had done to her. She had shrunk smaller and smaller, and she didn't know how else to react to anger anymore.

She had a visceral knowledge of how quickly a man's anger could turn to violence, and some cowering survival mechanism had been triggered in her that she didn't know how to undo.

Tenn stepped between her and the stranger, and she felt a new jolt of fear. Zeke's response would have been to fight fire with fire, to spit back with his own rage, his own threats. But when Tenn spoke, his voice was calm, even friendly.

"You're right about the stray dogs. My little girl is six, and I don't let her out our front gate alone. A friend of hers was walking with her big sister not too long ago and got bit. She needed ten stitches. It's a shame some people let their dogs run loose.

"Thing is, that storm last night brought a tree down on my friend's fence. This dog belongs to my little cousin. That little boy lost his dad this year, and it would break his heart to lose this dog. We'll get that fence fixed up, and I give you my word that this dog won't get out again."

The man on the porch grunted, grumpy but placated.

"Hurry up then. Get your dog out of my yard."

He walked back inside, and Tenn turned to Lani with a grin.

She wanted so badly to kiss him in that moment, and that terrified her. That fear snuffed her desire out as quickly as it had flared.

She turned back to the trap and pulled at the front, trying to figure out how to open it.

"Let me see," Tenn said gently. He knelt beside her and had the door open a moment later.

Dio sprung out and slammed into her, knocking her backwards and covering her face with slobbery kisses.

"Okay, okay!" She pushed him off, laughing. "It's good to see you too."

"Do you have a leash?" Tenn asked.

"Yeah." She reached beneath her oversized t-shirt and unclipped the leash that she had wound around her hips like a belt. They got Dio leashed and off of the property - much to the other puppy's dismay - and headed for home.

A quick message to the *Finding Dio* text thread the neighbor kid had started had the whole crew waiting at the Kealoha place when they got back. Kai greeted his dog with happy tears that were immediately replaced with slobber, and the whole mood was celebratory.

"Will you stay for lunch?" Emma asked Tenn and the neighbor kids. "I made a bunch of food for our family, but they ran off to help clear a road before I had the chance to offer them any."

The kids were quick to say yes to food, but Tenn gave Lani a questioning look.

A soft smile pulled at her lips as she gave him a bare hint of a nod. Far be it from her to keep chasing this man away. If he wanted to stick around knowing full well what she was going through, that was his business.

"I'll help," she said, turning back to Emma.

"No." Her eyes flicked from Lani to Tenn and back again, and her smile turned sly. "You've done enough today, rescuing Dio. Rest for a minute before you have to leave for work. The food's made, I just need to serve it up. Cody, would you set up that folding table?"

"Sure." The lanky teenager picked up one of the long tables they had used for Rory's birthday party.

"Thanks. Piper and Paige, why don't you run next door and see if your mom can join us for lunch?"

Lani wandered off around the side of the house, conscious of Tenn's presence as he walked nearby, to her left and just a step behind. Mostly she felt ill at ease when a man walked behind her. When Tenn did it, she felt like a queen with her own personal bodyguard.

She stopped in front of the 'ohana. A huge *lanai* surrounded the sweet little one-bedroom place where Adam and Emma used to stay every summer. No wonder Emma had spent the past few months pretending it didn't exist. Living in Uncle John's house must be hard enough without revisiting what was basically their honeymoon spot.

The house was half eaten up by weedy vines and the mosquito screens had mostly rotted away, but the place wasn't in terrible shape.

"I'm going to live here," she said, speaking the words aloud even before she had made a conscious decision. "I'm going to fix this place up for me and Rory."

"Can I help?" Tenn stepped up to stand beside her, leaving a scant inch of space between his arm and her shoulder. Lani could feel the heat coming off of him, a pleasant contrast to the cool shade and ocean breeze moving through. She turned and looked into his eyes.

"Why?"

"Why do I want to help you?" He made it sound like a ridiculous question. Maybe it was. But in the world beyond Pualena, she had learned that not everyone offers help out of the goodness of their heart or the joy of giving. That spirit of *aloha* could be found anywhere, but not everywhere. Some people, when they offered help and shelter, expected your heart and soul in return. Zeke had wanted to own her. And her baby.

She just nodded, looking him in the eyes. "Why?"

"I don't know, Lani. Why is your uncle out clearing a road he doesn't live on? Why did you spend your morning looking for Kai's dog?" He laughed and ran a hand through his hair. "Why did I tutor you in precalc like it was a part-time job? It's just what people do."

"Not everyone."

"You're home now. You don't have to do this alone anymore."

Without thinking, she reached up and touched his face.

Surprise flashed through his eyes, and a hesitation - wondering if he was misreading her, maybe. Slowly, he brushed a strand of hair out of her face. His thumb traced the curve of her cheek.

When she didn't pull away, his gaze softened. He kissed her, his lips barely brushing hers before he straightened up again.

It wasn't enough.

Lani took a step closer. "Kiss me again."

Tenn's smile lit up his face. She only saw that beautiful grin for a split second before his lips were on hers, fierce this time, a promise that she wasn't ready to wrap her head around. This time, she was the one to step back.

"Be patient with me?" she asked. Her hands still rested on his chest.

"Lani King, I'll be whatever you need me to be. We can take this as slow as you like."

She pressed her face against his chest, and he put his strong arms around her. They didn't crush or constrict. She didn't feel suffocated, like she had for so many years.

She just felt... held. Supported.

Loved.

28

Emma

Nearly one hundred sunrises had passed them by since they came to the Big Island. Emma had risen to greet most of them, sipping her coffee or milking the goats as pink and orange swept across the sky in slow motion. But she had never driven the short distance down to the sea cliff to watch the sun crest the horizon. Until today.

She rose and dressed in the dark, leaving the lights off to avoid waking Kai, who had climbed into her bed around three in the morning.

As a rule, Dio wasn't allowed in her bedroom, but today she patted the quilt, inviting him to jump up and sleep beside his boy. He hesitated for a moment, incredulous, then jumped up onto the bed and stretched out, pressing his back against Kai's.

"Good boy, Dio," she whispered. "Don't eat the cat."

Purring, Zuko climbed into the warm valley created by the sleeping giants and sprawled out on top of them. It was such a cozy scene that Emma was tempted to climb back under the covers, but she headed out through the dark morning and climbed into her car.

The neighborhood was already stirring and she passed other cars along the main road, all of them driving towards town and the highway. She was the only one headed down to the water.

Or not quite, she realized when she reached the tiny gravel parking lot and saw two other cars. Fishermen, maybe, or campers.

She closed her car door quietly, mindful of the sleeping households on either side, and walked the short path down to the coast.

They were well above the water here, some ten or twenty feet above the ocean on these black lava-rock cliffs that stretched for miles along the coastline. Not so high that bigger waves didn't splash up over the edge and fill small pools with sea water.

The air here was filled with a moving mist, the tang of salt and rock and ironwood groves.

She found a high, dry place to sit and watch the stars blink out of sight one by one.

Today she wore Adam's old hoodie the right way round, and in the front pocket she carried a small lacquered box. She sat with both hands in the front pocket of the hoodie, tracing the familiar lines of the wooden box with her fingertips.

Her sisters had held back a portion of Adam's ashes on the day of the paddle out, when most of them were scattered at sea. They were hers to keep, to lay to rest, whatever she chose. It had felt right to bring some small piece of him to Hawai'i.

She had thought to scatter the last of Adam's ashes here, in this bit of the Pacific where his father moved among the currents. But sitting here now, scattering the last of his ashes at sea didn't feel like the thing to do. So she just sat there, two hands on her husband's tiny urn, watching the sunrise.

There was a bare smattering of clouds out over the water, and a golden glow washed over them as Hawai'i turned towards the sun. The sky grew lighter, brightening almost to white before settling back into a bright blue.

It was less spectacular than she had imagined, nothing like a Kona sunset. But just as beautiful, in its way. A quiet awakening.

When the sun grew warmer and her thoughts turned to children and goats, Emma retraced her steps and reclaimed her car. On her way back up the main road, a sign caught her attention. It advertised fruit trees for sale: *ABIU, GUAVA, JABOTICABA*.

She pulled over.

Five minutes and thirty dollars later, she got back in her car with a healthy young jaboticaba tree.

It was Adam's favorite fruit, and one of the few that John hadn't planted in his orchard. The Brazilian grapetree took years to produce, and John had focused his efforts on the many tropical plants that produced a bounty almost overnight.

It would take a few years, but jaboticabas produced an abundance of delicious fruit. Best eaten fresh, they were like giant concord grapes that grew directly out of the trunk of the tree.

Back home, she put the tree in a sheltered spot and went inside to check on Kai. He was in the kitchen with Rory and Lani, who was frying fresh eggs in bacon grease. The sizzling aroma and warmth of the kitchen greeted her like an embrace as she closed the back door against the morning chill.

"Auntie!" Rory crashed into her legs. "Where'd you go?"

"Mom, look!" Kai grinned at her. "I taught Diogee a new

trick!"

"Let's see," she encouraged him.

"Dio, down," he told the dog.

Quick as a trained collie, the pup dropped to the tile floor.

"Up!" Kai said, and Dio sprung to his feet.

"Down," Kai said a moment later, and he was on the ground again.

"Good boy!" Kai mimicked him, dropping on his belly and going nose to nose with the dog. "You're such a good boy!"

"Such a good boy," Rory repeated, giving him a full strip of bacon.

Lani laughed. "With rewards like that, it's no wonder he's so trainable."

"He's the smartest boy," Kai crooned, rubbing his face against Dio's.

"He's a lucky dog," Emma said.

"We're the lucky ones," Kai insisted. She couldn't argue with him.

"I'm going to go see to the goats," she told them.

Outside, she brought the goats a few treats from their favorite trees, but she didn't get right to milking. With their overgrown babies still in there with them, there was no real hurry. It was past time to find new homes for the young goats, but that was a task for another day.

Farm chores stretched out ahead of her from now til eternity, and she found surprising comfort in that. There was always purposeful work to be done, always a reason to keep going.

For now, she had a tree to get in the ground.

She chose a choice spot in the front yard and cleared one of the huge, bushy, sunflower-like plants that the goats loved to eat. In the new open space, she dug a hole deep enough for the jaboticaba.

At the bottom of the hole, she placed the small box that held the last of Adam's ashes.

The Pacific had most of him, out flowing free with his mother and father. She would keep just a bit of him to herself. Here, on the island where he was born, on the land that had been left to their son. What better marker than his favorite fruit tree?

She would tell Kai someday, when the tree was a steady column crowded with shining fruit. For now, it was just for her.

She mulched the soil all around the sapling and watered it well, then went inside to eat the breakfast that Lani had made.

The kids had already eaten and gone next door to Tara's place, and she could hear their happy shrieks through the window as they jumped on the trampoline. Dio whined pitifully at the kitchen door, but there was no going outside unleashed for him until the fenceline was fixed.

"I've been thinking," Lani said slowly, picking at her bowl of sweet potato and eggs.

Zuko yowled, and Lani scooped him up off of the kitchen floor. He lunged for her bowl and took a big bite of egg yolk.

"You've been thinking?" Emma prompted when she didn't follow up right away.

"I'd like to fix up the guest house. Is that offer still open? Me acting as caretaker when you go back to California and rent out the main house?"

"I don't think we're going back to California," Emma told her.

It felt strange to say. She hadn't given the decision much thought since moving here. She had just let things unfold, and the island had welcomed them.

Leaving now, when her son was thriving and she had found some sense of purpose in caring for this place, would have felt deeply wrong.

"You're staying?" Lani's face lit up and she grabbed her hand, but a moment later worry flickered across her face. "Do you still... can we...?"

Emma squeezed her hand. "Lani, I would love for you to fix up the *'ohana*. Or stay in the big house with us, whatever you'd like."

"We're overdue for a home of our own, I think. It would be good for Rory and me to have our own little cottage. But I'm so glad you're staying. Really, I wouldn't want to live farther from you than across the yard. And it means the world to me that Rory and Kai get to grow up together, just like me and Adam."

"Same." She squeezed Lani's hand one more time, then stood and cleared the breakfast dishes.

"What are your plans for today?" Lani asked.

"I have seeds to plant. But before the garden and after the goats, I think I'll take some time to work on the cactus grass. There's a lot to clear before we can stretch the new fence."

"Are you sure you don't want me to do that? I can get out the weed whacker after work. It's so much quicker than your hand scythe."

"You have enough on your plate without taking on the cactus grass."

"If you say so." Lani glanced at the clock on the stove. "I should get ready."

"Go ahead. I've got the kids and the farm covered." Emma walked out the back door and looked out over the land, green and shining from the soft rain that had fallen all night.

Once the goats were taken care of, she put on the jumpsuit

that she used for prickly yard work. She walked out to the shed and stood there for a long while, looking between the hand scythe and the gasoline-powered weed whacker.

Power tools had been Adam's domain. She hated the noise and the violence of them. But the truth was, she couldn't clear the fence line with a hand scythe. The grass at the front would grow back in the time that it took her to work her way to the other end.

She picked up the weed eater and went outside to blaze a trail.

29

Tara

The sun was setting as Tara ran through the last of her evening chores. A thick layer of rainclouds lay over Pualena, giving them a rare purple sunset. The sky overhead glowed a dusky lavender, tinting everything below a strange and shadowy hue.

The evening milking was already done, with cow and goat milk both strained and stored in the fridge. All of the animals had clean water, and everyone that needed to be in for the night was.

With all of that taken care of, Tara decided to use the last of the light to do a bit of weeding in her overgrown garden. She loved her cucumbers and tomatoes, but with so many animals it was hard to find time for it all.

The life she had made for herself was filled with never-ending work, and she wouldn't trade it for anything. There was nothing more fulfilling than growing her own food with her children by her side. And she loved her animals, even the ones who gave her no eggs or milk in return for the absurd amount of money that she spent on feed.

"Hey Mom?" Paige rattled the fence that kept the animals out of the garden (well, most of the animals most of the time). "Have you seen my riding helmet?"

"You didn't hang it up by the door?" Tara stood and stretched her aching back.

"I thought I did, but I can't find it."

"Did you look in the car?"

"It's not there either."

"I'll help you find it before we leave tomorrow."

"But I want it tonight," she insisted. "I wanted to draw on it with my new sharpies."

"I'll come help you look in a few minutes." She hefted the pile of weeds that she had pulled and tossed them over the fence into a wheelbarrow. Here in the tropics, she never bothered with formal compost piles. This batch of weeds would go under the banana trees, where the chickens would root through them and the rain would melt them to fertilizer almost overnight.

"Dinner will be ready soon. Cody and I made Nana's chicken pot pie."

"You're a rockstar."

"I know." Paige ran off towards the house, and Tara heard the kitchen door slam when she went inside.

She smiled and crouched back down to start on another row.

Before she dug in, she called her husband and ran a cord from her phone to her ear so that she could keep weeding while they talked.

Idle hands were a foreign concept to her; she couldn't just sit and talk on the phone. At least not without feeling like she wanted to crawl out of her skin.

"Tara, hi," he answered on the second ring. "I've been

meaning to call you."

"It's been a few days." She had been meaning to call him too, but life got in the way and before she knew it he had already been gone for a week.

They had discussed - for all of two minutes - the whole family going to the mainland together. But between the cost of five roundtrip tickets and the thought of finding someone to take over the daunting list of farm chores, family vacations weren't really on the table.

"How are you?" He sounded odd, but then again it was already late at night on the east coast. He was probably just tired. "How are the kids?"

"All's well here, just a normal week for us." A moment after she said that, she frowned. She probably shouldn't say that as if their lives were no different without him... but that was the truth of it. Mitch commuted to Hilo and worked long hours, then collapsed onto the couch when he got home. If anything, this past week with him gone had felt smooth and easy.

The kids had been happier without his loaded questions about schoolwork or his ill-tempered snapping. Cody had even played board games with her and the girls in the evenings instead of retreating to his room like he normally did.

What did it say about their family, that everyone was happier with him gone?

Maybe they had just needed a bit of a break.

"How was your reunion?" she asked, a solid minute too late. "That was tonight, right?"

"It was yesterday." His voice was heavy. Unease prickled through her chest. She sank back on her heels, giving the conversation her full attention.

"And you fly out tomorrow?"

"About that..." He cleared his throat. "I'm not ready to come back just yet."

She straightened up and brushed the dirt from her hands. "What about work?"

"I hate that job." The vehemence in his tone surprised her. He'd hated driving a UPS truck the last few years he'd worked the route, but he'd been over the moon when he landed the manager position a few years back.

"Mitch, what are you saying?"

"My first day back, I ran into... I reconnected with Stacy."

It took a few seconds for the name to find purchase. "Your highschool girlfriend?"

"Yeah." He sounded miserable. "We're, um, we're gonna give it a chance."

Her knees gave out slowly, and she sat on the wooden corner of one of her raised beds.

"My mom's not doing well, so I thought I should stay in town for a while anyway. You know, stay close. Help her out."

Tara stared into middle distance as darkness swallowed the garden.

"Are you still there?" he asked.

"Are you saying that you want a divorce?"

"We don't have to decide now. We can just... take some time."

She squeezed her eyes shut and tried to take a breath. He wanted to see how things worked out with his old flame before he decided if he wanted to stay married to her or not.

Who *was* this man? How had she ended up with him?

She could hardly remember who he used to be.

"We haven't been happy together for a long time," he said. "Isn't it about time we admitted that?"

She opened her eyes and looked up at the moon. It floated

just above the tops of the ohia trees at the back of the property, almost full. Then the clouds shifted again and swallowed it whole. The color had drained from the sky, leaving just a trace of purple against the black.

"I am happy," she said weakly. A quiet protest. "I love our life."

"You love *your* life," he shot back. "You love the kids and that money pit of a hobby farm. But you're not actually happy – not when I'm home, at least." The bitterness faded into something small as he said, "You don't need me."

"The kids need you. Your son needs you."

"They don't need me. They have you."

"How can you say that?"

"I'm not abandoning them," he said, a little too forcefully. "I'm right here. It's not like they have to worry about missing school. They can come visit whenever they want. Get to know their grandparents while they're still around."

"Mom?" Paige's voice rang through the dark. "Where are you?"

"I'm here," Tara called back. In a quiet voice she said, "I have to go. We can talk later."

"Fine." He sounded tired, defeated. Like *she* had left *him*.

Then again, maybe she had. For so many years, she had tried to pull him into games with the kids, cooking together, digging in the garden. And year after year, he had retreated. Eventually, she stopped trying.

She had found her own happiness in a life that ran parallel to his.

The call disconnected and she stood, moving slowly as she left the garden and closed the gate behind her.

Maybe they had left each other a long time ago.

"Look!" Paige said when she walked through the kitchen door. "I found my helmet!"

She held it up and showed her the silver cartoons that she had drawn on the dark purple riding helmet. As desolate and adrift as Tara felt in that moment, she had to smile.

It wasn't just her daughter's artwork – though the cartoon ponies prancing around the brim of the helmet were certainly worth a smile. It was the whole scene.

Cody stood at the stove, cutting into the chicken pot pie that he had made from scratch. When he was as small as his sisters, he'd helped Tara make that exact recipe dozens of times. Now he could make it himself, letting Piper and Paige be the ones to help.

Paige sat at the kitchen counter, her brow furrowed in concentration as she added more ponies to the brim of her riding helmet. Piper was a few feet away on the living room floor, using their old German Shepherd as a pillow and reading a Nancy Drew book.

She felt a warm certainty that everything she needed was already right here.

...and then, in the next moment, the cold fear of how she would maintain it without her husband's support.

She veered away from the kitchen and walked down the hall.

"Mom?" Cody called after her. "Are you okay?"

"Dinner smells amazing," she called back over her shoulder. "I just need to wash up."

She walked past the bathroom and into their little home office, where she logged into the family computer. She went to the website for their local credit union to check the balances on the joint accounts that she shared with Mitch.

He was still using their checking account, she noted. A hefty bar bill from the night before, and another from a diner that morning.

There wasn't much left... and their savings account wasn't much better.

They lived comfortably - but like most people, they lived paycheck to paycheck. There was a small cushion for emergencies, but it wouldn't hold out long.

The property was paid off, which was a blessing. But the monthly cost of feed required to keep the animals alive was high... not to mention bills and lessons and everything else that kept their life going. Mitch might not have been a very active participant in their daily life, but he had supported their family financially for nearly twenty years.

Tara slumped back in her chair, fighting off a spinning-falling-sinking feeling that threatened to overwhelm her.

What was she going to do now?

The story continues in *Big Island Neighbors*,
available January 27th 2024.

Acknowledgments

Christine, you showed me what was possible and gave me the courage to build a new life from the ground up. I am so endlessly grateful for your generosity and advice. Thank you.

Alison, you made me believe that I could actually make a living at this writing thing. Thank you for encouraging me to write this book. I adore you.

Hali'aaloha, thank you for helping me get the details right. I'm so grateful that you took the time to read this book and share your thoughts. *Mahalo piha.*

Dad, thank you for always being there. You can knock him down, you can drag him down, but you can't keep a good man down. Surf City.

Mom, thank you for your steady encouragement and top-notch proofreading. I love you.

Teresa, thank you for being a true friend through the hardest year of my life. Your adventures in Mexico are a real-life embodiment of what these books are about: women starting fresh and creating their own best lives time and again.

Britt, you're the sister I found on the Big Island. I miss you.

Dayna, thank you for answering my livestock-related questions. The life you've built for yourself is inspiring, and so is your open-hearted generosity.

Jesse, thanks for encouraging me to keep writing. Too bad this book doesn't have enough murder, mushrooms, and mayhem for you to actually read it. I'll circle back to that epic fantasy series eventually, I promise.

Gigi, thank you for always giving us a safe place to land. I love you up to the angels.

Made in United States
Troutdale, OR
08/12/2024

21940185R00159